BROKEN

Other titles by Penny Kendal

Christina's Face
The Weekend Ghost

BROKEN

Penny Kendal

Andersen Press • London

For my sister Debbie

First published in 2003 by
Andersen Press Limited,
20 Vauxhall Bridge Road, London SW1V 2SA
www.andersenpress.co.uk

British Library Cataloguing in Publication Data available
ISBN 1 84270 174 6

Typeset by FiSH Books, London WC1
Printed and bound in Great Britain by Mackays of Chatham Ltd., Chatham, Kent

Chapter 1

'Give it to me!' Rebecca demanded. 'Come on, Jack. You'll break it!'

They were standing in the room – the one room Caroline had said was strictly out of bounds. Rebecca had only come in after Jack, to get him out. But what a room – it was like some kind of museum. The surfaces of the dark wooden sideboards and tables were covered with china figures – ladies, fancily dressed as if they were arriving for a dance.

And now one of them *was* dancing. Jack had picked it up – a beautiful lady, with a long, silky blue dress. He was twirling her in his hands. Rebecca felt as if the eyes of the other ornaments were watching, begging her to do something.

'Jack! It's not a Barbie doll, you know. It's not plastic!'

The figure was smaller than a Barbie and very much more fragile.

'Jack! Give that to me, or put it back. Let's get out of here. Caroline will go mad if she finds us.'

'All right. Come on.' But Jack had a worrying sparkle in his eye. He dodged past her, out of the room, still swinging the figurine in his hand.

'Jack! No!'

He was already through the kitchen door and out

onto the sunny patio. Rebecca caught up. She snatched at the figure. Jack stepped back, glaring at her. But as he did, his foot caught on a loose paving stone. He tripped.

Rebecca tried to grab the figure, and then Jack, to keep him upright. But she was too slow. The china lady shot out of Jack's hand. It hit the patio with a heartbreaking crack, and shattered.

At that moment Rebecca could have sworn she heard a high-pitched scream. Or was it only a seagull's cry? Jack had landed on his bottom and sat surrounded by fragments of china. Only the head was still in one piece, the blue eyes staring up at them accusingly.

Jack swore. 'You idiot, Becca! I never would've dropped it. It's your stupid fault.' He stood up and brushed himself down.

'It was *you* who took it,' Rebecca said angrily. 'What did you have to do that for? Why did you have to go in that room in the first place?'

'I heard her,' said Jack. 'Caroline – she was in there before, when I came downstairs. I peeped round the door and she was dusting those ornaments – and she was *talking* to them. Honest, she was, Becca. So I wanted to have a closer look, that's all.'

'Talking to them?' said Rebecca. 'Don't be daft. And if you'd looked and not touched then *this* wouldn't have happened, would it?'

For a few seconds they both stood staring at the shattered pieces in silence, as still as if they were ornaments themselves.

‘Do you . . . d’you reckon we can fix it?’ Jack asked, but the glimmer of hope in his voice tailed off, even as he spoke.

‘Fix it!’ Rebecca sneered. She crouched down and picked up the disembodied head. The face was so delicately painted, the skin tone looked almost transparent. The head had been slightly tilted on the figure, as if it was shy or sad. It was certainly sad now.

‘Caroline’ll kill us,’ Jack suddenly croaked, ‘won’t she, Becca?’

Rebecca thought about Caroline, the aunt they’d only met for the first time that morning, the aunt whose collection of china figures was as precious to her as children. That’s what Mum had said.

‘Well I’m not hanging around to find out,’ said Jack. He took one look back towards the kitchen door and began to run down the garden.

‘Jack! You moron! Where do you think you’re going? It’s no use running away!’

Jack had disappeared through some overgrown bushes. Rebecca hesitated. She didn’t see why she should stay there and take the stick. Honestly, Jack was more like a five-year-old than an eight-year-old, the way he behaved. She hurried after him, working her way with difficulty through the brambles. The garden clearly hadn’t been looked after for years.

She found Jack crouching in a small potting shed.

‘I’m not coming back,’ he said stubbornly.

He tried to pull the door shut, but Rebecca blocked it with her foot. ‘She’ll never let us stay now – you know that, Jack, don't you? Not after this.'

'So?' Jack shrugged. 'We'll have to go home. I don't mind. Caroline's a silly cow anyway.'

'Are you thick or something? We can't go home. Mum's not there. She has to stay in that clinic till…'

'Till what?'

'Till she's off the heroin, that's what. If we can't stay here we'll end up in care. We won't be by the sea like this.'

Rebecca felt her throat tighten. Going into care was her worst nightmare. Mum had been dead set against it too.

'It's the only option, love,' Denise, the social worker, had said. 'Unless you've got any family who could take them?'

That's when the shock had come – Mum suddenly announcing that she had a sister – just like that, out of the blue. She'd never even mentioned her before.

'Her name's Caroline,' Mum told them. 'And she lives by the sea. You'll like that. It'll be a holiday.'

It turned out Mum hadn't spoken to Caroline since before Rebecca was born, which was more than thirteen years, but she wouldn't say why.

'Oh, y'know – stuff,' was all Rebecca could get out of her.

Caroline had taken a lot of persuading to have them stay. Rebecca had heard Mum on the phone. 'Please, Caro. They're good kids. They'll be no trouble. It's only for three weeks.'

Rebecca hadn't wanted to go. She'd begged Mum to let her stay with a friend instead, but no one would have Jack. And Mum wasn't going to let him go to Caroline's on his own.

'Who knows what he'll get up to if you're not there keeping an eye on him,' Mum had said. 'You know how he is.'

Rebecca knew how he was. She'd always had to keep an eye on Jack. Mum wasn't with it most of the time.

'Put that back!'

Jack was sniffing at a rusty bottle with a 'keep out of reach of children' label. He'd probably have drunk it if she wasn't there.

Jack pouted.

Rebecca glared at him. 'We could be on the beach now if you hadn't had to go mucking about in that room.'

She thought back to their arrival. She'd been so anxious, but when she'd seen the big house – and how close it was to the beach, her hopes had risen. And Caroline had seemed okay. She'd smiled at them, even if it did look like it took some effort, and she'd made them a major lunch – a proper cooked meal. They'd done their unpacking and had been about to ask if they could go down to the sea, when Jack had sneaked off, through the forbidden door.

What would happen now? If Caroline wouldn't let them stay, Mum might come out of the clinic early. Then she'd never get off the smack. They'd probably end up in care anyway. Rebecca felt the tears welling up behind her eyes. She rolled the china head in her hand – the smooth face, the sharp cracked edge of the broken neck. It wasn't just the figure that was broken. It was Mum. It was everything. It was their life.

She yanked Jack up. 'Come on. We'll go back to the house and tell Caroline what happened. We'll clear up the mess and say it was an accident. We'll say we're sorry.'

'She'll kill us,' Jack protested.

'Well, if she's going to kill us I'd rather die quickly than wait here on death row.'

'We could do a runner – go to the beach,' Jack suggested. 'We could hide in one of those beach huts. You know – you can see them from your window.'

'And then what? We'll have to face her sometime, Jack. Come on.'

'Oh all right.' Jack sighed.

He followed her slowly back through the bushes. Would Caroline forgive them? It was hard to tell. To look at her, you'd never have thought she was Mum's sister. She was tall, well built, with thick dark hair, and much older than Mum – in her forties, probably.

Rebecca's T-shirt caught on a bramble. She swore. Jack overtook her as she disentangled herself. She caught him up on the overgrown lawn, but he suddenly came to an abrupt halt. Rebecca pushed at him crossly, but his stiffness made her follow his gaze towards the house. A dark shape was moving in the doorway. Before Rebecca had time to blink, Caroline was outside. Her old-fashioned summer dress billowed in the breeze, making her look larger than life. Rebecca felt her heart lurch.

But Caroline was walking towards them, waving.

'Oh, there you are! I wondered where you'd got to...'

Then she froze. Her foot had crunched on something. Rebecca heard it. She watched, aghast, as Caroline looked at the fragments on the patio. At first she didn't seem sure what they were. Then she reached down. She picked up a shiny blue piece from the figure's dress. Her face hardened and went white. Her eyes and mouth seemed to double in size as she looked up at Rebecca and Jack.

She screamed.

Chapter 2

Rebecca had never heard anyone scream like that. It was so loud, so painful, so *devastating*. Mum hadn't even screamed that loud when Jack had been playing with matches and set fire to the sofa. Jack hadn't screamed that loud when Mum's boyfriend Mitch hit him with his belt. It was as if when she'd looked down Caroline had found a dead body – not some smashed bits of china.

Maybe Jack was right after all. Maybe she was going to kill them. Rebecca looked nervously at Caroline, who was leaning against the wall of the house, gasping for breath.

She pulled Jack towards her. 'It was an accident,' she pleaded. 'Jack only wanted to have a look. We never meant anything to get broken. We're sorry, aren't we, Jack?' She shook Jack, who mumbled something. 'You don't know how sorry we are,' Rebecca continued. 'We'll do anything to make it up to you, won't we, Jack?'

Caroline straightened and swung round to face them.

'Go to your rooms!' She spat the words out so fiercely that drops of spit landed on Rebecca's face. 'Go to your rooms, this minute!'

'But . . . ' Rebecca tried again, 'it was an accident – we . . . '

'I said, *go to your rooms*!'

They went.

Rebecca climbed the two flights of creaking stairs, with Jack following close behind. It was incredible to think of one person living alone in a house this size. Caroline had said it used to be a guesthouse. But that was no explanation for why she was living alone in it now. When Rebecca thought of their cramped, poxy council flat, it made her sick.

She felt a moment's longing for the house they'd lived in before. It wasn't big and old like Caroline's, or small and grimy like the council flat. That house had been perfect – modern, with just the right amount of space and a lovely garden. It was over two years now since they'd had to move. She'd thought that was the worst time of her life. She hadn't known then that there was worse to come.

Jack followed her into her room.

'Go to your own room,' Rebecca told him, but he was already making himself comfortable in the only chair.

'I don't want to be on my own in there. It's boring.'

'If she finds you in here she might get even madder.'

Jack shrugged. 'She never said we couldn't stay though, did she? You said . . .'

'She's probably on the phone right now trying to get us put in care.'

That shut Jack up. Rebecca walked to the window and looked out at the sea and the bobbing sailing boats. She hoped she was wrong.

Sighing, she sat down on the old iron bed, and opened her hand to look again at the china head. The eyes seemed to glare at her like Caroline had. She turned it face down. 'Caroline must hate us now. If only we could get her another one or something.'

Jack sat forward, eagerly. 'Yeh, do you think you've got enough money?'

'I haven't got a penny. Mum was skint. She said to ask Caroline for some money and that she'd pay her back later. Caroline's not going to give us any now, is she?'

'What about the money you were saving up? Didn't you bring it?'

Rebecca felt her body tense. She rolled the head back and forth in her hand. 'Mum nicked it,' she said finally, without looking up.

'Your money?' Jack looked shocked. 'I never knew she took that.'

'She couldn't help it, Jack. She'd take anything to get the money for the next fix.'

Rebecca had been saving for new trainers. Hers were embarrassing beyond belief. She'd nearly had enough to get the ones she wanted. But when she'd looked, the money had gone. She'd straightaway assumed it was Jack. She'd have accused him too, if Mum hadn't come in and seen her searching the drawer.

'I ran short, love, I just had to borrow a bit. I meant to tell you. Don't you worry – you'll get it back.'

Rebecca had wanted so much to believe her. She'd wanted to think that the money was for the rent, or food or the electric bill – not for drugs, and that she would get it back, like Mum said.

'We could steal some money,' Jack suggested. 'If we get it off Caroline then it won't really be stealing because we're going to get something for her with it anyway.'

'Jack!'

'Mum did it, didn't she? She stole your money.'

'But that was different – it was only because she was desperate. She needed the money for heroin. She couldn't help herself.'

Rebecca hated to think how Mum had got the money to keep buying drugs. She must've done worse things than taking Rebecca's savings – that was for sure. There was the time when she'd seen Mum with three expensive-looking sparkly tops laid out on the bed. Mum had said she got them cheap at the market. They looked so nice, that the next day when Mum was out, Rebecca had been tempted to sneak into Mum's wardrobe and try one on. To her surprise, the tops had gone. She'd asked Mum, and Mum said crossly that she'd decided she didn't like them and had taken them back. And she'd had a go at Rebecca for going in her wardrobe.

Rebecca hadn't known about the drugs back then. It was only much later that it occurred to her Mum might have been shoplifting – and selling stuff on. It was a horrific thought. Rebecca still didn't want it to be true. But Mum must have been getting the money from somewhere.

'Why couldn't she just stop doing the drugs, Becca?' asked Jack. 'Why did she have to go in that place and we had to come here? I want to go home. I want it to be you and me and Mum and no drugs and no Mitch. Just us. Caroline hasn't even got a telly,' he added in despair.

'If Mum gets off the drugs – and if she stays off them, then it will be like that,' said Rebecca, aware that there were a lot of 'ifs'. 'And Mitch is in prison anyway. He won't come near us again.'

'But why did she have to go there? Why couldn't she just stop?'

'I don't know, Jack,' Rebecca said in frustration. 'She tried, didn't she? You saw what it was like. She needed help. Sometimes people can't stop by themselves.' Rebecca sighed.

'Here – give us a look at that head,' said Jack.

Rebecca was only too glad to stop talking about Mum and drugs. She held it out.

Jack grinned. 'It looks well weird without the body.'

'You'd look well weird without your body too! I think we should keep it. Then we might be able to find another one the same, and get it for Caroline when we've got the money.'

'What d'you think they cost?' Jack asked.

'No idea,' Rebecca said miserably.

Half an hour later they were both bored to tears. Jack was pacing round the room for the umpteenth time. Rebecca felt like throttling him.

'I'm starving,' Jack moaned. 'How long's she gonna make us stay up here? We might die of starvation and someone will find our skeletons in a hundred years' time.'

'It's not like the door's locked,' Rebecca reminded him.

Jack rushed to the door and peeked out. 'I can't hear anything. She's probably gone out. I'm gonna creep down to the kitchen and get some grub. I'll be mega quiet – she won't know.'

He looked at Rebecca as if daring her to stop him.

'Let's wait a bit,' Rebecca said. 'She'll probably come up soon. You don't want to get in more trouble, do you?'

Jack smirked and put one foot defiantly out of the room.

'If you're going, then I suppose I'll have to come with you.' Jack and kitchens were a dangerous combination. She put the china head down on the bedside table and followed Jack cautiously onto the landing.

As she started down the stairs, a floorboard creaked loudly.

'Ssh!' Jack hissed.

They stood still – listening. Nothing. Rebecca didn't like the silence. She wished they had some clue to where Caroline was, so they could be sure to avoid her.

They stopped once more as they approached the kitchen. Not a sound. They edged into the room. It was empty. Jack instantly relaxed and went straight for the fridge.

'There isn't much in here,' he commented. 'Mostly fruit and lettuce and stuff. D'you want a yoghurt?' He held up a pack of four.

Rebecca nodded doubtfully.

'D'you think there's some crisps somewhere?' he asked her. 'Have a look, will you?'

Rebecca opened a cupboard. It was full of saucepans. Jack pulled himself up onto the work surface, and began to explore the top cupboards. 'Best things are always in the top cupboards,' he told her.

'That's only when someone's trying to keep them away from their greedy kids,' Rebecca pointed out. 'Get down. You'll leave footprints.'

She thought back wistfully to the treats Mum used to surprise them with from the top kitchen cupboard at home. The little chocolate chip cakes had been Rebecca's favourite. But that was a long time ago. Lately the cupboards at home had become emptier and emptier. Half the time they'd existed on chips from the freezer.

'Nothing here, anyway,' Jack said, jumping down. 'Nothing we'd want. Try over there, Becca. Hurry up, will you, she might come.'

They ended up with an unsliced wholemeal loaf, a packet of plain biscuits, and the yoghurts, some butter and cheese from the fridge. Rebecca found a plastic bag under the sink and put the stuff into it, along with some plates and cutlery. She handed the bag to Jack, and filled two glasses with orange juice.

They started up the stairs. There was still no sign of Caroline. As they reached the first landing, Rebecca thought she heard something. She nudged Jack and he stood still. Yes – there it was again. It sounded like a cat mewing. But Caroline didn't have a cat, did she? Perhaps it was a stray that had got shut in, and couldn't get out.

Rebecca put the glasses down on the next step. 'Wait here,' she whispered to Jack. She couldn't bear the thought of an animal being in distress.

The sound seemed to be coming from behind a door that was almost, but not completely, shut. She pushed the door gently, just wide enough to see through. The sound got louder. The room was small and square, with bookshelves, and a desk with a computer and a telephone. In the corner was an armchair, on which was curled, not a cat – but Caroline herself.

Rebecca stared. Caroline had her legs and feet tucked up on the chair, her arms hugging her knees, like a small child. And she was sobbing, big convulsive sobs, each ending with a tiny cat-like cry.

Chapter 3

Rebecca stood staring open-mouthed at her sobbing aunt. What should she do? Jack was nudging her impatiently from behind. She let the door slip silently back and turned to him.

Jack met her eyes, his face questioning and bewildered. She pointed up the stairs, and then held her finger to her lips to keep him quiet.

She sighed with relief as they reached the bedroom.

'Come on then, tell me,' said Jack, closing the door. 'What was going on in there?'

'It was Caroline. She was crying,' said Rebecca.

'*Crying*?'

'Yes, that's what I said.'

'But why?'

'Probably because you broke her precious ornament, that's why!'

'Grown-ups don't cry about things like that.'

Jack looked thoughtful. 'She must be off her head. That must be why Mum never talked to her for years. Mum sent us to stay with a mad woman, Becca. That's what she's done. I want to go home.'

'Mum wouldn't have sent us here if Caroline was really mad,' said Rebecca, but she wasn't as sure as she'd tried to sound. The heroin had stopped Mum thinking straight. Maybe she'd forgotten what Caroline was like, or been too desperate to even care.

'I suppose I ought to go in there, and try to talk to her,' said Rebecca, aware that this was the last thing she felt like doing.

'Nah – she'll only start yelling again,' said Jack. 'Let's eat something. We might as well, now we've got it.'

Rebecca lay in bed later that evening, exhausted but wide-awake. Jack was finally asleep in his room. Caroline hadn't come up, and Rebecca hadn't plucked up courage to go down and speak to her. It was hard to imagine anyone getting that upset about an ornament. Rebecca was used to Jack breaking her things, and she still got mad with him – but Caroline – screaming and then sobbing her heart out – that was weird.

Rebecca tossed and turned. She wished Jack hadn't chosen that smelly cheese. Neither of them had eaten it and it was stinking the room out. She pulled the duvet up over her head, trying to pretend she was back home and Mum was fine and everything was going to be okay. But this place was too quiet to be home – she'd never been anywhere so quiet.

What was Caroline doing now? And what was going to happen to them? She'd never let them stay after this. She'd probably get a social worker to come in the morning to take them away.

Rebecca felt the heat of her breath building up under the duvet. It was too hot, but she didn't move. She'd known before they arrived how important it was to keep Jack under control. It was Jack getting into trouble that had put social services on to them back home. He'd been playing up at school – and he'd been late a lot too, even though Rebecca had tried her best to get him up and there on time. Mum hardly ever got up in the mornings and she'd kept missing meetings that had been arranged with Jack's teacher.

In the end a social worker, Denise, had come round to see what was going on. Denise had been keeping an eye on them since then – and they'd lived with the fear of being taken into care.

Rebecca pushed the duvet down and a surge of cooler air leapt into her ears. She thumped her head back on the pillow. If only she could have stopped Jack going in that room. If only...

Rebecca must have fallen asleep eventually. She woke in the morning with a feeling that she was being watched, and opened her eyes to see the piercing blue eyes of the china head staring back at her from the bedside table. The whole face seemed far more lifelike than yesterday, giving her a creepy feeling, as if the broken head had a mind, a brain – and was really looking at her. She shuddered.

'Becca! Come on, wake up!'

She rolled over to see a dishevelled-looking Jack leaning over the other side of the bed.

'At last! I've been up for ages.'

'Have you seen Caroline?' Rebecca asked anxiously.

'No, but I've heard her. She's downstairs talking to a man.'

'A man? Do you think he's a social worker?'

'I dunno. I'll go down and see if I can hear what they're talking about, if you like?'

'Let's get some clothes on, then we'll both go,' said Rebecca.

Her stomach groaned, and it wasn't hunger – it was despair. This was a nightmare. Why did Jack have to go and break that figure? She gave him a furious look.

'We won't really go in care, will we?' Jack asked. 'They won't split us up, will they?'

'I hope they do,' Rebecca said spitefully.

Jack's eyes met hers – glassy and hurt.

'I didn't mean it,' said Rebecca. 'Just go and get dressed, will you?'

Jack went and Rebecca sat up and turned to look at the china head. The eyes seemed full of interest, as if it had been listening – and was waiting to see what was going to happen next. She turned quickly away, and heaved herself out of bed. She jerked with a sudden pain in her right hand. 'Ow!'

She rubbed her hand, and clenched and unclenched it. What was the matter with it? To her relief the pain gradually eased off as she washed and dressed.

Jack's face peered round the door. 'You ready?'

Rebecca inspected him. He'd put on the same shorts and T-shirt as he'd been wearing the day before.

'Couldn't you wear something different?'

'I like these,' Jack insisted. He sniffed. 'It stinks of cheese in here.'

'Yes, we'd better take this stuff down.' As Rebecca gathered the leftover food back into the plastic bag, her hand twinged violently. 'Ow!'

'What?' said Jack.

'I've got cramp in my hand. I must've slept on it or something.' Again, she rubbed her hand for a few seconds and the pain eased.

With trepidation, they started down the stairs. Rebecca wished she'd had the courage to go and talk to Caroline last night. She might have been able to persuade her to give them another chance.

They had reached the first landing, when a sudden loud noise made them both jump. It sounded like *drilling*.

Rebecca looked over the dark wooden bannisters. The sound was clearly coming from the room with the china figures. What was going on in there? The noise stopped abruptly. She saw the door moving slowly back and forth, but no one came in or out. Then the drilling started again.

'What do you . . . ' she whispered to Jack, but he had gone. She turned to see that he was already at the bottom of the stairs, in the hallway, heading straight for that room – the room where it had all begun.

'Jack! No!'

As she rushed after him, a man with grey hair suddenly appeared in the doorway. He held his hands out to stop Jack.

'There'll be no more going in that room for you,' he said gruffly. 'See this?' He reached into the room and picked up a screwdriver, pointing it directly at them. Rebecca and Jack both stepped back fearfully.

The man turned and pulled at the door, fiddling with a brass plate, which he then began to screw into ready-prepared holes.

'Your aunt's asked me to put a lock on this door. Keep you out. See?'

So this was the man Jack had heard Caroline talking to. And he wasn't a social worker. Rebecca felt a flood of relief.

The man suddenly gave a loud grunt and looked towards the kitchen. Rebecca's body stiffened as she turned to see Caroline in the kitchen doorway. She was wearing a black dress, which, combined with her miserable expression, made her look as if she was in mourning.

'They haven't been...?' she began. Her voice was croaky and tired, as if she hadn't had much sleep.

'No – don't you worry,' said the man. 'I've been standing guard all right. Mind you, it's about time you had a new lock on this door – with all those valuables in there. If I were you I'd put them ornaments in glass cases. Wouldn't need dusting and it'd be much safer.'

'No, no,' Caroline said firmly. 'Lock them up in cabinets? That would be like... No, I certainly couldn't do that. Are you nearly done, Bill?'

'Yes, nearly there now.'

Bill screwed the final screw and then tested the lock. He handed the key to Caroline, who stood clutching it tightly. She hated them – Rebecca could feel it. She gave Jack a dig in the ribs. 'You've got something to say to Caroline, haven't you, Jack?'

'Yeh, ermm... I'm sorry I broke your lady. I never meant to. It was an accident. You're not gonna kill us, are you, or put us in care? It was me who took it but Becca did make me break it – trying to get it off me...'

'Look, err, I think I'd better be off now,' said Bill, winking at Caroline.

'Thanks for coming so quickly, Bill,' said Caroline.

He picked up his tool bag and Caroline showed him out of the front door.

Rebecca and Jack stood between the kitchen and the newly-locked room, waiting for her to come back to deal with them. But she didn't stop when she reached them. She hurried past into the kitchen.

Rebecca watched and then nervously followed her, with Jack close behind. Was she really not going to say anything about the china figure?

'I see you helped yourselves to supper,' Caroline commented, speaking directly to them for the first time that day. 'I hope you didn't eat all the bread and butter?'

Jack reached into the bag that Rebecca was still holding. 'The butter's melted,' he said, 'and the bread's a bit . . . ' He held up the ragged loaf.

'Hmm, well, never mind.' Caroline took the bag from Rebecca and pulled out the cheese. 'I think this Stilton's had its day. I should have thrown it out ages ago. Put it in the bin, will you, Jack.'

Jack screwed up his face. Rebecca didn't want any trouble. 'I'll do it,' she said. She walked over and dropped the cheese into the bin. As she did, something inside caught her eye. Fragments of china, all in a heap. She stared guiltily at the tiny pieces. It was awful to think of Caroline out on the patio sweeping her treasured possession into a dustpan and tipping it into the bin.

What was Caroline playing at? Why wasn't she laying

into them about it? The new lock – did that mean she was letting them stay? Surely she wouldn't have bothered with it otherwise. This thought gave Rebecca hope. But if they were staying, she wished Caroline would just tell them off properly and then forgive them.

They ate breakfast silently. Rebecca's hand started throbbing, but she dared not mention it.

Finally Caroline spoke. 'I have a lot of work to do today,' she said stiffly.

'What do you do?' Jack asked.

'I write history books.'

'Bor...' Jack began, but Rebecca nudged him before he could get to the 'ing'.

'Books?' she said quickly, trying to cover for him. 'That must be very interesting.'

'So I think the best idea is for you to stay out of the house,' Caroline continued, without looking at them.

'Can we go to the beach?' Jack asked the burning question.

'You can do what you like,' said Caroline, 'as long as you behave, and don't bother me.'

Rebecca shifted uncomfortably on her seat. She was relieved to know for sure that Caroline was letting them stay. But she clearly couldn't stand the sight of them after what they'd done.

'Should we come back for lunch?' Rebecca asked hopefully.

Caroline considered this. 'I'd make you some sandwiches, but I'll need to get more bread...Tell you what, get something while you're out, then you needn't bother me.'

'We haven't got any money,' said Jack.

Rebecca felt herself blush with shame. 'I think Mum forgot to give us some,' she explained. 'If you could lend us something, I'm sure she'll pay you back.'

'Like heck she will,' Caroline muttered. But she reached for her bag and pulled a ten-pound note from her purse.

'Here you are. Make it last.'

'Oh, thank you,' said Rebecca. If they could manage not to spend it – or to spend as little as possible, then they could save towards another figurine for Caroline. They *would* get her one. Rebecca was determined.

Chapter 4

Out of the house, along the lane, they ran down the steep path to the beach.

'Wait for me!' Rebecca called.

Jack had charged ahead of her, and was jumping down from the promenade to the beach, roaring with delight. Rebecca breathed deeply, drinking in the sea air, staring in awe at the expanse of beach and rippling sea. From the bedroom window it had looked like a painted picture but now she was standing in it. It was real.

She slipped her feet out of her sandals and tiptoed over the strips of cool pebbles and sand, to join Jack at the water's edge.

'It's freezing!' Jack cried out happily, jumping over the little waves. They walked along the beach for ages, letting the waves wash over their legs, so that they lost all sense of time. The beach gradually became busier, with family groups dotted around, and they had trouble finding where they'd left their shoes.

'Here they are!' Jack called. He pounced on his shoes and then collapsed onto the sand. Rebecca flopped down beside him.

'Ouch!' she yelled. As she'd sat down she'd put her weight on her right hand and the pain had started again – a sharp jab, followed by a dull throbbing ache.

'What's the matter?' said Jack.

Rebecca rubbed her hand. 'Nothing. My hand's playing up again, that's all.'

'D'you think it's broken?' Jack asked.

'No – it's not that bad. I thought I'd just slept on it, but it's weird that it's still hurting now.' She rubbed her hand gently. 'It'll be okay.'

'I'm dying for a drink,' said Jack.

'I'll get some,' said Rebecca, 'but we'll have to make them last.'

She was reluctant to break into the ten-pound note at all and chose the cheapest drinks on offer at the beach stand – small cartons of orange squash.

'I wish I had a bucket and spade,' said Jack. 'I'd make the best castle ever.'

'I'd get you one but I want to save the money.'

'For a stupid ornament?'

'We've got to stay with Caroline for three weeks – it'll be hell if she hates us all that time. Don't you want to make it up to her?'

'We don't even know what they cost or where you get them,' Jack protested. 'We might never save enough money and even if we do, we might not find one. Then it'll be a waste.'

He had a point. But he hadn't seen Caroline sobbing in that chair. Rebecca would never forget that sight.

'We've got to try,' she insisted.

Jack shrugged sulkily and began to dig a hole in the sand with his hands.

Rebecca lay back, looking up at the blue sky with a few tiny lost-looking wisps of white cloud passing over. She drifted into a wonderful daydream. Mum was with them on the beach, relaxed and smiling.

'*Are you with this boy?*'

Rebecca sat up sharply. A plump woman whose shorts and T-shirt looked several sizes too small, was clutching an unhappy-looking Jack by the arm.

'What's happened?' Rebecca asked. Why had she taken her eyes off Jack?

'I didn't do *nothing*,' Jack seethed.

'Din do nothing!' the woman repeated, mockingly. 'What do you call stealing a spade from a three-year-old then?'

'Oh, Jack, you didn't?' Rebecca cringed with embarrassment.

'My son's over there, wailing his heart out in his dad's arms,' the woman continued, pointing with the spade.

Rebecca turned to see the distraught, red-faced child, who was watching them over his dad's shoulder, in between bursts of raucous crying.

'Where are your parents? I want to speak to them,' the woman demanded.

'They're not here,' Rebecca said awkwardly. 'Jack's very sorry, aren't you, Jack?'

'I never stole it – I only borrowed it,' said Jack. 'That kid weren't even using it.'

'No parents?' said the woman. 'Someone must be with you.'

Other people were beginning to stare. 'Just say sorry, Jack,' Rebecca begged.

'Sorry,' Jack said furiously, wrenching himself away from the woman.

'No one seems to care what their kids get up to these

days,' the woman muttered. She shook her head in disgust as she walked back to her husband and son.

'Oh, Jack,' said Rebecca, sighing in despair.

'It's only 'cos you wouldn't get me a spade,' Jack reminded her.

'Shut up, Jack.'

'I'm hungry. Are we gonna get something to eat or do we have to starve while you save up for a stupid china Barbie?'

'I said *shut up.*' Rebecca closed her eyes and put her hands over her ears. But she knew she couldn't make him disappear. She couldn't even keep him quiet.

They left the beach and walked into town. Rebecca bought some cheese and tomato sandwiches from a grocer's shop, and they sat down on the edge of a green where people were picnicking.

'I hate tomato,' Jack protested. He pulled the slices out of his sandwich and held them out to her. The juice and pips dripped down her leg.

'*Jack!*'

Rebecca pulled her sandwich out of the plastic wrapper. At least her hand wasn't hurting now. That was something.

Nearby, a man and woman with three children were tucking in eagerly to chicken drumsticks, crisps and mounds of cherries. Rebecca looked around at the other picnickers. Families – she suddenly realised. They were all happy-looking families.

'Mum should have asked Dad to let me stay with him,' Jack said miserably. 'That would've been better than staying with "crazy Caroline".'

'I don't think Mum even knows where he's living,' said Rebecca.

She felt bitter when she thought of Gary. He was Jack's dad, not hers, but her own dad hadn't even hung around to see her born, so Gary was the only dad she'd ever known. They'd been a family once. Not that they'd ever gone on picnics. She watched jealously as the man with the three children handed out cans of Coke.

She'd called Gary 'Dad' back then, but she thought of him only as Gary now. If he hadn't done a runner and gone off up North with another woman, everything would have been different. They wouldn't have had to move to that grimy estate. Mum wouldn't have got so low – and she'd never have ended up with Mitch.

Jack grabbed at a clump of daisies. 'Why can't we have proper parents like normal people do?' He pulled the petals off viciously.

Rebecca sighed. 'Just luck of the draw, I guess.'

They finished eating and wandered up the high street, looking in shop windows and watching enviously as luckier children came out with bulging plastic bags and cheerful faces.

'Can't we just . . . ?' Jack began, eyeing a beautiful model sailing boat in one window.

'If we go in, you'll only start wanting things you can't have,' said Rebecca. She'd already spent half the money. Caroline had said 'make it last' but she hadn't said for how long.

Jack pouted. 'Let's go back to the beach, then. This is boring.'

Rebecca shook her head. 'I don't want to bump into that woman again.'

'*I want to talk to your parents*,' Jack mimicked. 'I wish I'd told her the truth. That would've shut her up. My dad ran off when I was six and my mum . . .'

'I'm glad you didn't,' Rebecca interrupted.

She'd never told anyone the truth about Mum and she was sure Jack hadn't either. Not even her best friend Nikita knew the truth. Luckily Nikita wasn't one to ask lots of questions, especially with her dad being a policeman. Mum was using, not dealing, like Mitch, but it was still illegal, wasn't it? If the police had found out, she could have gone to prison too.

'If we're not going to the beach, then what are we doing?' Jack whined.

'Wait, look,' said Rebecca. She'd stopped outside a shop. The shabby green sign read *Bygone Days – Antiques and Collectables*.

Chapter 5

They peered through the window at the mass of strange objects cluttering the dark shop – lacy lampshades, jugs with faces, glass vases, teapots, books.

'You don't want to go in there, do you?' said Jack.

'They might have a figure like Caroline's,' said Rebecca.

'I can't see any,' said Jack. 'Come on, let's go.'

'Maybe I should go in and ask.'

Jack made a face. 'If you want.'

Rebecca hesitated, unsure if she had the courage. She'd never been in an antique shop.

'Will you wait out here?' she asked. The last thing she wanted was Jack breaking anything else.

'All right,' said Jack, 'but be quick.'

Rebecca pushed the door gently and a bell rang in the shop. She was greeted by a musty smell, and a man with a kind face and a greying-blond beard, who came out from a room at the back.

'Can I help you, love?'

Rebecca shifted uncomfortably, her eyes wandering among the flowery cups and saucers that lay before her on a table.

'Erm . . . do you have any china ornaments?'

The man pointed to some small china animals.

'No – err, not like those – people – ladies.'

'Let me have a look for you,' said the man, stroking his beard thoughtfully.

He reached behind him and picked up the figure of a small china woman standing by a well. Beneath the well were the words 'A gift from Cromer'.

Rebecca looked doubtfully at the figure as he handed it to her. The woman was squat, cheerful and brightly painted. This was nothing like Caroline's Ladies. Caroline would probably hate it. But the label on the bottom said five pounds. That was the exact amount she had. Perhaps it would do – as an apology. At least Caroline would know they'd tried. But then again, she'd also know it was her money they'd spent on it. She might be angry.

Rebecca couldn't decide. She glanced at the window to check that Jack was still there. He had his face pressed up against the glass, watching her, his nose squashed flat and his cheeks and mouth distorted. She turned back to the man, but luckily he didn't seem to have noticed.

'I don't think it's really what I'm looking for,' she told the man, handing the figure back.

'I'll give it to you for £4.50?' he offered.

Rebecca shook her head. She was distracted by Jack's goggly eyes, and worst of all, he had his tongue out and was smearing the glass.

'No thanks. I've got to go.'

She hurried out of the shop, the bell ringing behind her.

'Come on, Jack, you're disgusting.'

'You didn't get it then?'

'It wasn't right. Maybe I'll come back and show that man the head, so he knows what we want.'

'If you must,' said Jack. 'Did you see that boy in there?'

'What boy?'

'The boy with red hair. He was watching you from that room at the back – staring at you.'

'I never saw him.' Rebecca felt uneasy. She didn't like the thought that someone had been watching without her knowing. She turned to Jack. 'I hope he didn't see you making those stupid faces.' She made a face at him, imitating his earlier efforts.

Jack laughed and made a face back at her.

They were both tired and hungry by the time they got back to Caroline's. When she opened the door to them her eyes were narrow and hostile. She didn't ask anything about their day or what they'd been doing. She just told them coldly to go and get cleaned up for dinner.

Rebecca climbed the stairs heavy-heartedly. Jack headed for the toilet while she went into her room. The late afternoon sun was casting a beam right onto the bedside table, where the china head sat glistening. Rebecca picked it up and stroked the golden painted hair, as if trying to comfort it, like she wished she could comfort Caroline; like she sometimes wished someone would comfort her. She would definitely take it into that antique shop tomorrow. They must cheer Caroline up somehow.

'What you doing?'

It was Jack. Embarrassed, she reached to put the head back down. She stopped and stared at the bedside table. There was a deep scratch in the wooden surface – just where the head had been standing. She was sure that scratch hadn't been there before.

'Did you do this, Jack?'

'What?' Jack came over to see. He felt the scratch with his finger. 'I never did that. Why do you go blaming me for everything? If it weren't there before, you must've done it yourself.'

But Rebecca knew she hadn't.

'Caroline will think we're set on breaking everything,' she said crossly. 'Do you think we should tell her? She might be more angry if she finds out later.'

'No way – she'll only go berserk again. I'm going down now.' Jack stomped out of the room.

Rebecca looked again at the bedside table. The surface was completely smooth apart from that one scratch. She glanced at the china face in her hand, and felt a strange sensation. She was sure there was something different about it. She brought the head up to eye level. The face was as eerily lifelike as it had been that morning. Then, for a split second, the expression seemed to change. The face looked angry. Rebecca shuddered. She rubbed her eyes. The face couldn't really have changed. Yet there was definitely something creepy about it. The broken neck edge looked sharp enough to scratch the table if someone pressed it down really hard. But why would anyone do that?

She put the china head into the top drawer and pushed it tightly closed.

Chapter 6

'Why haven't you got a telly?' Jack asked Caroline, as they sat awkwardly in the lounge after a tense meal.

'I don't feel the need for television,' Caroline said sharply. 'I prefer to read.'

Jack looked appalled.

Caroline gave him a thoughtful glance. 'I have a box of children's books somewhere – that were mine and your mother's. I'm sure you'll both find something to keep you amused in there. Wait and I'll fetch them.'

Caroline left the room.

'I hate reading,' moaned Jack.

'You'll have to pretend then,' said Rebecca.

Jack yawned loudly.

When Caroline eventually returned she was carrying a dusty cardboard box.

'See what you can find in there,' she said. She put the box down in the middle of the floor and made herself comfortable in a big armchair, with a very heavy-looking book.

Jack eyed the box warily as if it was about to explode. Rebecca knelt down and pulled out the first two books. She didn't recognise the titles, so she chose the one with a more interesting cover and began to read. At least it would help to push Caroline and Jack out of her mind for a while.

When she looked up after a few minutes, she saw that Jack had most of the rest of the books out of the box, and was making a castle with them. Typical. At least he was quiet. She glanced nervously at Caroline, but she seemed to be engrossed in her book.

The quiet didn't last long though. Jack's castle was clearly under siege and he couldn't resist making the sound effects.

'*Boom! Pow!*'

'Jack, don't!' Rebecca whispered.

'I'm bored,' Jack complained.

Caroline glared at him. 'I think it would be better if you both went up to your rooms. You can take the books with you and leave me in peace.'

Rebecca gathered the books quickly back into the box and carried it upstairs, followed by a sullen Jack.

'I hate her,' Jack moaned, lying on his back on Rebecca's bed.

Rebecca was sitting on the floor, searching the box for a book that Jack might be persuaded to look at. He wasn't a good reader but she had to keep him occupied somehow.

'Look at this,' she said, suddenly.

'I don't want to read a stupid book,' Jack protested.

'This one's not a book, it's a photo album.'

Jack slithered off the bed and came to see.

Rebecca's fingers tingled as she turned the stiff, plastic-coated pages. She felt an inexplicable guilt – as if the album was private and they shouldn't be looking at it. But Caroline had given them the box. She couldn't mind, could she?

'It's just photos – we don't even know who they are,'

said Jack, glancing without interest at a picture of a girl holding a baby.

Rebecca studied the picture more closely. The girl looked about her own age and was smiling shyly at the camera. 'It must be Mum and Caroline,' she told Jack, excited as the realisation struck her. 'Look – the girl is Caroline and the baby must be Mum.'

Jack laughed. The baby in the photo was bald and had a very screwed-up face. 'Really? I've never seen a picture like that of Mum.'

Thinking about it, Rebecca realised she'd never seen any photos of Mum as a child at all. Why did Mum have no photos?

She turned the album pages. Here was a later photo when the baby was about two, and the older girl about fourteen. They were on the promenade by the beach – sitting in front of a bright blue beach hut. Behind the children were two adults in deck chairs, a man and a woman. The man didn't look well – he had a thin face and shrivelled skin, and his body looked slumped in an uncomfortable position. He was smiling though. The woman looked younger than him, and had a serious expression.

Jack crouched down to look. 'Who are they?' he asked, pointing to the adults in the picture.

'They must be our grandparents,' Rebecca said. It felt odd to say the word 'grandparents' and to see these two strange faces staring up at them from the page.

'They're dead, aren't they?' said Jack.

Rebecca nodded. 'Isn't it weird that Mum's never shown us any photos? Not even of her parents.'

'She never told us she had a sister, did she?' said Jack. 'It's not like it's something you'd forget.'

'I don't think I'll forget *you* in a hurry,' Rebecca teased.

Jack hit her playfully.

Rebecca pushed him off. 'I wish we could talk to Caroline and find out what happened between them.'

'I'll ask her, if you like?' said Jack.

'I'm not sure. She might throw another wobbly or something. Something bad happened, don't you think? It must be bad if Mum's never told us.'

'We can show Caroline the photos,' said Jack, 'and get her to tell us about them. She gave us the box, didn't she? She can't blame us for wanting to know.'

'Maybe we should wait and ask Mum,' said Rebecca.

'Mum never told us before,' Jack pointed out.

Mum. Rebecca's thoughts turned to her and her stomach tensed. When would Mum phone? She wished she could to speak to her – just to know she was all right. Mum had said it would be awkward for them to phone her but she'd said she would phone them after a few days – give them and her a chance to get settled first.

She wondered if Mum was feeling any more settled than they were. And how was she going to be when she came out of the clinic? Would she be off the drugs for good? Or would it start all over again?

'Do you think Mum'll be okay?' Jack asked, reading her mind.

'I hope so,' said Rebecca, but Jack was looking at her anxiously. The fear she felt in her bones and her heart was reflected in his face. She forced her mouth into a smile. She mustn't let Jack see how scared she was. 'Mum will be fine – don't you worry.' She took a last glance at the photo of Mum as a baby, and snapped the album shut.

Chapter 7

The next morning Rebecca was up and dressed before Jack. She opened the bedside drawer and reached inside to take out the china head. Where was it? She couldn't feel it. Surprised, she pulled the drawer further out and reached right to the back. Nothing.

She had put it in there, hadn't she? Could Jack have taken it out last night? She reached right to the back of the drawer once more. In the far back left-hand corner, she felt a nick in the wood. She pushed her finger into it. Yes – it was a hole.

She pulled the drawer right out. She could see the hole clearly now – round and slightly larger than the china head. She pushed the drawer back in and pulled out the second drawer. There it was – the head. The face was looking up at her mockingly. It was as if it had deliberately played a trick on her by rolling to the back of the drawer and falling through the hole to the drawer below.

'Don't be so silly,' she told herself. She picked up the head, and had another look at the hole in the top drawer. Had it been there before? It must have been. She eyed the scratch on the top of the bedside table. The scratch and the hole must both have been there before. There was no other explanation.

Jack came into the bedroom, already dressed.

'Wow! Clean clothes,' Rebecca teased. 'You'd have started to pong if you'd worn those shorts and T-shirt another day.'

Jack avoided her eyes. Rebecca could tell something was wrong.

'What?' she askcd.

'My top clothes are clean,' said Jack, 'but I'm out of clean pants. I had to put on yesterday's.'

Rebecca suddenly remembered something she ought not to have forgotten. Mum had been very behind with the washing, and although Rebecca had been trying to keep up with it herself, on the day they'd left they were very short of clean clothes. Mum had said to take the dirty washing in a plastic bag and to ask Caroline to put it in the washing machine for them.

Rebecca hadn't liked to ask Caroline about the washing when they first arrived, and after that she'd completely forgotten about it.

'Why didn't you remind me, Jack?'

'I forgot.'

'We'll have to ask her,' said Rebecca. 'I just hope she doesn't go mad.'

'I wanted to ask her about the photos,' said Jack.

'You'd better leave that till later,' Rebecca told him.

Downstairs in the kitchen she held the washing bag awkwardly. 'We've got some washing,' she told Caroline. 'Mum didn't have time to do it before we came. Is it okay if we put it in your machine?'

Caroline frowned. For a moment Rebecca thought she was going to say no.

'Put it in the machine and I'll run it later,' said Caroline. Her voice was not friendly but she didn't sound angry either.

She waved her hand towards the little room by the kitchen where the washing machine was kept. Rebecca breathed a sigh of relief and took the washing through. It was only as she reached down towards the washing machine door, that she realised she was still clutching the china head. She put it down on top of the washing machine while she opened the door and pushed the washing in.

'I've made you some sandwiches,' Caroline announced as Rebecca came back into the room. 'And there's an apple for each of you and a fruit juice. So you shouldn't need to bother me.'

She met Rebecca's eyes with a look that said clearly – stay out of my way and out of the house for as long as possible.

'Thank you,' said Rebecca. At least they wouldn't have to spend money on lunch.

After breakfast they were about to leave the house, when Rebecca remembered the head. She'd been holding it. Where was it? She retraced her movements in her mind. Then she realised – she'd left it on the washing machine. What if Caroline saw it? She might think they'd put it there on purpose to upset her.

Rebecca whispered to Jack in the hallway.

'I'll get it,' he said, and before she could stop him he was creeping round the kitchen door.

He was back in an instant. 'It's all right. I got it. I don't think she saw. Come on, let's go.' He handed the head to Rebecca and she slipped it into their lunch bag.

'If we *have* to go to that shop again,' said Jack, 'then I'm coming in with you this time – you can't stop me.'
'All right,' said Rebecca. 'Just don't touch anything.'

The man with the beard gave a smile of recognition as Rebecca entered the shop.

Jack followed her, and his arm knocked against something metal. 'Be careful,' she whispered.

Jack gave her a scowl and clasped his arms against his chest.

'Changed your mind, did you, love?' the man asked, picking up the 'woman and well'. 'You're in luck, I haven't sold it yet.'

'No, no,' Rebecca said awkwardly. 'I'm looking for something more like this.' She pulled the head out of the lunch bag and held it up. The man took it and examined it carefully.

'We want one with a body as well,' Jack added helpfully, swinging his arm precariously close to a crystal vase.

'You do, do you?' said the man, reaching out to steady the vase. He brought the head up close to his eyes. 'And how did you come by this?'

Rebecca gave Jack a 'keep still' look, and then turned back anxiously to the man. 'We're staying with our aunt and we err...we accidentally broke one of her ornaments.'

'She went crazy,' Jack added. 'I don't know why – she's got a whole room full of them. She shouldn't mind about just one.'

The man looked at them, a flicker of interest in his

eyes. 'Your aunt wouldn't happen to be Caroline Walters, would she?'

Rebecca felt her face redden.

'Do you know her?' Jack asked. 'I think she's nuts.'

'Jack!' Rebecca gave him a dig in the ribs.

The man laughed. 'Yes I know her. She's one to keep herself to herself, mind you. She does come in here sometimes. Historian, isn't she? I know she's keen on antiques – collects china figures. That's what made me think of her. Never knew she had any family though.' He looked at them curiously.

'We're staying with her while our mum's...in hospital,' Rebecca explained.

'Yeh – worst luck,' said Jack.

'We want to get her another figure like that one,' Rebecca said, 'to make it up to her. Are they very expensive? You see, we don't have much money.'

'That depends,' said the man. 'It's hard to identify this just from the head – any marks would be on the bottom, you see. You'd have to leave it with me and I'll do a bit of research for you.'

Rebecca hesitated. 'You won't tell Caroline, will you?'

'You have my word.' The man smiled and winked.

At that moment Rebecca caught a glimpse of movement from the back of the shop. She looked up to see a tall boy with red hair move quickly out of sight. So that was the boy Jack had seen yesterday. He was watching again. Rebecca felt irritated. Eavesdropping – that's what that boy had been doing and it wasn't nice.

'Come back tomorrow and I'll hopefully have an answer for you,' the man suggested. 'But I have to warn you – it looks like a good piece. It could be pricey.'

Rebecca turned back to the head, which was sitting in his open right hand. The face looked beautiful now, like it had when she'd first seen it on the figure. Did it keep changing, or was it her imagination?

'That's that,' Rebecca said miserably, as she and Jack walked down the road towards the beach. 'I bet it cost her loads. No wonder she was upset. I wish there was some way we could get her one.'

'We'll have to wait till we're rich,' Jack suggested. 'When I'm a famous footballer and you're... a TV star.' He looked thoughtful, as if caught up in this fantasy future. 'Mind you, Caroline might be dead by then,' he added.

Chapter 8

Unsure what to do, they decided to walk as far as they could along the promenade. It was cooler today – not sitting on the beach weather. Rebecca shivered in her T-shirt. She wished she'd put on something warmer.

The promenade was lined with brightly coloured beach huts, and Rebecca read the names to herself as they passed.

'*Puffin, Huffin, Catnap, Seagulls, Silver Spray, Plaice and Ships, Dolphin, Swan's Nest.*'

'I wish we had one of those,' said Jack. 'Just you and me – and Mum when she's better of course. We could sleep in it and everything. Then we wouldn't have to stay with Caroline.'

'I don't think people stay in them,' said Rebecca. 'They just use them in the day, to get changed for the beach.' It was a nice idea though. Rebecca wondered what Mum was doing now. She had visions of a long hospital-like ward with all the patients lying in white beds with white sheets. They'd all be sick and shaking like Mum was when she tried to come off the drugs herself. It was a horrible image.

They walked a long way.

'The trouble with this place is there's nothing to do,' Jack moaned. 'It's not like other seasides where there's loads of arcades and stuff.'

'I like it better like this.'

'You would.'

But Jack was in luck. At the end of the promenade they came to a pier and an amusement arcade.

'Give us some money, Becca,' he said. He was already through the door and pulling levers and pushing buttons frantically.

'You can have a pound and that's it,' said Rebecca. 'I don't want to spend all day in here.'

She gave him the money and he changed it for smaller coins. Then he ran excitedly from one machine to the other. Rebecca followed at a distance, and watched as Jack shot at villains on a screen with a realistic-looking rifle.

'That one was Mitch!' he told her, as a villain dissolved into a splatter of red on the screen.

Rebecca couldn't help smiling. 'I'll have a turn after you.'

Jack shot unsuccessfully at a few more, and then watched as Rebecca grabbed the rifle and hit two evil-looking villains in quick succession. Splat! Splat! One for Mitch and one for Gary, she thought to herself, but she didn't say it out loud. Gary was Jack's dad after all.

'Can I have some more money?' Jack begged.

'All right,' she relented. She gave him another pound and he headed towards a shooting cowboy game called Mad Dog McCree. She joined him and had a turn on that one too. Then he tried a machine full of tenpence coins on a ledge. It looked like one more coin would tip all the others over.

Rebecca leant impatiently against a wall as Jack bounded about.

'Come on, Jack.' She'd had enough now, and was ready to leave.

'No – not yet.'

At last he was down to two tenpence coins. He pushed the first one into the machine with the ledge. The coins looked so close Rebecca was certain they were going to fall. But nothing happened.

'Last go,' said Jack, pushing his other coin in. There was a loud '*Crash!*' They both jumped. Jack looked at the empty ledge with astonishment. He pushed his hands through the flap at the bottom of the machine. His eyes lit up as he pulled out handfuls of coins. 'I've won! Becca, I've won! We're rich!'

Rebecca looked at Jack's handfuls of coins and excited expression. 'You've won all right but we're not exactly rich,' she pointed out. 'They're only 10ps.'

'But there's tons of them!' Jack had begun stuffing them into their lunch bag, handful after handful – and there were certainly a lot. 'We can get a china lady if you want! And loads of stuff for ourselves!' he declared.

'You need to work on your maths,' said Rebecca. 'It can only be a few pounds you've got at the most.'

'But I'm gonna win more – loads more,' Jack said defiantly.

Rebecca couldn't help feeling tempted. 'Give me a few, then,' she said.

'Here you are.' He gave her a generous handful of coins.

She searched for a machine where the coins looked close to falling. Then she pushed her first coin in. She held her breath, willing the coins to tip over. Nothing happened.

She spent the money within seconds, winning nothing. She watched Jack for a while but could see he was pouring his winnings away too.

'Come on,' she said. 'We're going now. I've had enough of this place. You're losing all the money you've won.'

'I'm going nowhere.' Jack moved quickly away from her, deeper into the arcade.

'Jack – come on – we're going right now.'

Jack ignored her. He was pushing coins into another machine. Rebecca grabbed his arm and pulled.

'Get off me!' He pushed her hard so that she reeled back, bumping into a passing man who gave her an angry look.

'Sorry,' Rebecca said to the man. She stepped back crossly towards Jack.

'I've got this feeling,' said Jack. 'I'm going to win again, I know I am.'

'You won't, Jack. You'll end up with nothing.'

'You watch.'

Jack lost. He hit the machine in frustration.

'Why don't you bring the money you've won out on the beach and we'll count it up – see how much there is?' Rebecca suggested.

'When I win some more – then we can count it all,' said Jack. 'I'm gonna win enough so we can get something for you and something for me, and Mum of course, *and* a china lady for Caroline. *You* want to get one of them, don't you?'

'You can't win that much, it's impossible,' said Rebecca. 'I'm going, so you'd better come with me. *Now*, Jack!'

'*No*.'

Rebecca grabbed his arm tight and yanked him hard towards the door. He grasped hold of her hair and pulled. She swore at him and tried to wrench his hand off her hair. They twisted and turned and then tumbled and were rolling about on the cold hard floor.

Rebecca tried to untangle herself from Jack but he was angry now and was holding onto her arms, squeezing, not letting her up. He was yelling insults at her furiously. She got an arm free and hit him. Then she unwrapped her legs from beneath his and sat up, breathless.

She saw to her horror that a number of people were watching them with deeply disapproving expressions, and a slimy-looking attendant had come out of a booth and was heading towards them.

'What do you think you're playing at?' the attendant asked, sneering down his nose at them. 'This is an arcade not a wrestling ring. Out, now!'

'She started it,' Jack complained.

'It's all right – we're going,' said Rebecca. The humiliation was almost unbearable. She stood up quickly and brushed herself down.

'I'm not going yet,' Jack said stubbornly.

Rebecca looked at him in despair and disbelief. Why did she have to have such an impossible boy for a brother? The man was going to start asking where their parents were any minute. With this thought she unexpectedly began to cry.

'Do you need some help?' asked a voice behind her.

She turned. Standing there with a grin on his face, was the boy who had been spying on them from the back of the antique shop – the boy with red hair.

Chapter 9

Rebecca glared at the boy and then pushed past, out of the arcade.

'Hey, wait!' he called.

He was following her now. Rebecca felt furious. Then he overtook her and blocked her path.

'Leave me alone,' she said fiercely.

'Jeez, I was only offering to help, that's all. Your brother looks a bit of a handful.'

Rebecca met his eyes for the first time. They were large greeny-blue eyes. Were they mocking her? She wasn't sure. His cheeks were flushed and he still had that smarmy grin. It made her cringe.

At that moment Jack caught them up.

'I'm Charlie,' said the boy.

'I'm Jack and she's Rebecca,' said Jack. 'Do you live in that antique shop?'

'Not in the shop – behind it and upstairs. It's my dad's shop.'

'Thought so – I saw you staring at us in there,' said Jack.

Charlie's cheeks flushed red again. 'I wasn't staring – I was curious, that's all. We don't usually get kids coming in the shop on their own.'

'I'm not a kid,' Rebecca retorted.

'She's thirteen and I'm eight,' Jack told him. 'How old are you?'

'Fourteen,' said Charlie. 'My dad wasn't half chuffed about that bit of china you brought in this morning.'

'I don't see why – it's only a broken head,' said Jack.

'Must be something special for Dad to get all worked up like that,' said Charlie.

'I was winning loads of money so we can get Caroline another one,' Jack told him. 'She's our aunt and she's well-gutted about it. You should have heard her scream when it got broken . . . and later Becca found her *crying*. She's hardly talking to us now.'

Rebecca shrank back. She couldn't bear Jack telling him all their personal stuff. It was none of Charlie's business.

'How much have you won?' Charlie asked.

Jack scrabbled around in the bag, finally pulling out two tenpence coins.

'Is that all you've got left?' Rebecca asked in horror.

'That's why I needed to keep playing, so I could win more. It was you who came and ruined everything, Becca.'

Rebecca was too angry to speak.

Jack turned to Charlie. 'I bet you spend loads of time in that place. There's nothing else to do round here, is there?'

'Round here? There's enough to do – but it's not much fun on your own.'

Rebecca looked at Charlie. She'd give anything to have a bit of time on her own – without Jack. 'Haven't you got any friends?' she asked sarcastically.

'I live with my mum in Norwich, mainly,' said Charlie. 'All my friends are there. Dad moved here and got the shop when they split up. That was five years ago. Since then I've come here in the school holidays.'

'You're lucky,' said Jack. 'I never get to see my dad. I did used to see him though. Becca's never seen her dad. Not even *once*.'

'Jack! Will you shut up?' Rebecca cried.

'Why? I'm only being friendly. It's better than you.'

Jack suddenly touched his head and looked up. 'It's raining!' he announced.

'That's all we need,' said Rebecca.

'We'd better go back in the arcade,' said Jack. He raised his chin provocatively at Rebecca.

She raised her fist as if to hit him hard.

'You...you can come back to my place...if you want,' said Charlie.

'Have you got a telly?' Jack asked, a new glint of hope in his eye.

'Yes, of course. I've got loads of computer games as well.'

Jack's eyes lit up. He looked pleadingly at Rebecca. 'Come on, Becca. There's nothing else to do, is there? Which way, Charlie?'

Rebecca hesitated. She wasn't sure what to make of Charlie. Why did he want to hang around with them? Was he that desperate for friends? But going back to Caroline's was an even more depressing thought, and they had little money to do anything else. It was raining harder now. She could feel it trickling down the back of her neck. She shivered.

'Come on!' called Jack.

'All right,' said Rebecca.

Charlie led them quickly back to the high street and down an alleyway beside the shop. He showed them into a small lounge that was almost as cluttered with old things as the shop itself.

'Shift some of that stuff and make yourselves comfy,' said Charlie.

Rebecca carefully arranged some old magazines in a neat pile at one end of the sofa and sat down. She wiped the rain from her hair. She felt uncomfortably damp, and was already wishing they hadn't come.

They ate their packed lunches in front of the television. Charlie made himself a sandwich and joined them. When they'd eaten, Jack begged to see the computer. Charlie took them up to his room, which was small and crammed with boxes and files, most of which didn't look as if they belonged to him.

'This is my newest game,' said Charlie, holding one up for them to see. 'The graphics are incredible.'

'Can we play it?' Jack asked.

Charlie turned to Rebecca. 'Will you have a go?'

'It's all right. I'll watch.'

She would have played if it was with Nikita. But she didn't want Charlie showing her up. Anyway, she wasn't in the mood.

Charlie was soon engrossed in games with Jack. Rebecca sat sulkily on his unmade bed. Every now and then she caught Charlie looking at her, as if he was hoping she'd join in. She ignored him, looking around at the cluttered shelves. The lowest one had more than twenty old toy cars lined up on it.

'Bit old for toy cars, aren't you?' she commented.

'Them?' Charlie looked up. 'They're not toys – they're antiques. I've been collecting them for years –

Dad started me off. It's great fun going round the antiques fairs, hunting for a bargain. I've got the boxes for lots of them too.'

Rebecca gave him a look that said, 'Big deal.' What was so special about having the boxes?

He read her eyes. 'If you've got the original box, it makes the car worth much more – double sometimes,' he explained.

This sounded crazy to Rebecca. She made no comment.

Eventually Rebecca had to prise Jack away from Charlie and only managed it with the reluctant promise that they would see him again tomorrow.

'He's great!' Jack exclaimed as they walked along the road.

'You mean his TV and his computer games are great,' Rebecca sneered.

'Why don't you like him?' Jack demanded. 'He was trying to be friendly to you all the time and you hardly even talked to him.'

Rebecca wasn't sure why she had taken so strongly against Charlie. 'Don't you go telling him any more of our personal stuff, anyway. You've told him enough already.'

'I hardly told him anything. You're mad, you are.'

They had reached the gate and Jack rang the doorbell. Then he rang it again. Last time Caroline had taken a long time to open the door. This time she didn't come at all.

'Maybe she's out,' Jack suggested.

'That's great, that is.' Rebecca frowned and rang the bell for a third time.

'We'll have to go back to Charlie's,' Jack said eagerly.

'Oh no we won't,' Rebecca said firmly. 'Let's try round the back.'

They walked down the side of the house and through a second gate to the patio. The kitchen door was swinging open. Rebecca could hear Caroline's voice clearly from inside. They paused against the wall to listen. Rebecca couldn't tell who she was talking to, but it was instantly clear that she was talking about them.

'First my Arabella figurine and now this,' Caroline was saying. Her voice was bitter and furious. 'They're as bad as their mother, coming here and destroying everything. What could I have been thinking of, saying I'd have them? Steph always could wind me round her little finger. She had a nerve after all this time – and after what she *did*...'

Caroline stopped abruptly. Jack had been trying to shuffle closer to hear better and had knocked some pebbledash from the wall. She must have heard him. Rebecca gave him an irritated look. She wanted to hear more. What did Caroline think they'd done now? And what was it Mum had done?

Chapter 10

Rebecca pulled Jack quickly away from the wall, trying to make it look as if they'd just walked through the gate. Caroline's head appeared, looking round.

'We're back,' Jack told her.

'We rang the bell,' Rebecca explained, 'but no one answered so we came round . . . '

Caroline glared at them and Rebecca looked down to avoid her eyes. It was then that she caught sight of the kitchen floor, and gasped. The red tiles were under at least two centimetres of water. Caroline was paddling in it, leaning against a mop. There was a dark patch along the bottom edge of her dress, where the water had climbed up.

'I was otherwise occupied as you can see,' she seethed.

'It's a flood!' Jack exclaimed. 'Was it the rain, or did you have a burst pipe?'

Caroline gave a sharp intake of breath. 'The washing machine has flooded,' she told them. 'And I don't need to ask who's responsible for that, do I?'

'What do you mean?' Rebecca asked in bewilderment.

'Do you think I don't know what you've been up to?'

'We weren't up to nothing,' Jack protested. 'Were we, Becca? We've been out all day.'

'Messing about with the buttons, I shouldn't

wonder,' said Caroline, giving Jack a knowing glance. 'Don't think I didn't see you meddling in there this morning – *and* the speed you ran off. Up to no good, weren't you? Well?'

Rebecca was stumped. She couldn't explain about the head, but she didn't see why she and Jack should take the blame for the washing machine flooding. It wasn't fair.

At that moment, Bill, the man who'd put the lock on the door, appeared from the utility room. He was holding a basket of sopping, soapy washing. 'I can't see what the problem is, I'm afraid. You'll have to get a proper plumber to take a look tomorrow. I've rescued the washing anyway. Sorry I can't do more.'

Caroline sighed. She took the washing from Bill and pushed the basket towards Rebecca. 'If you want clean clothes you'd better take this lot to the launderette now.'

Jack screwed up his face. 'Not me – I don't have to go, do I?'

'Yes – both of you,' said Caroline.

'Can't we have something to eat first?' Jack begged.

'And I'm supposed to cook you something with the kitchen in this state?'

'We'll help you clean it up,' Rebecca suggested.

'No thank you very much.'

'It's not fair!' Jack protested. 'It wasn't our fault at all. You can't starve us because your washing machine's broken.' He turned to Bill for support. Rebecca thought she saw a flicker of sympathy in Bill's eyes, but he clearly had no intention of getting involved.

Caroline's voice rose in fury. 'Fine – you can get some fish and chips while you're out. Now out of my sight before I do something we'll all regret.'

She pulled another ten-pound note from her bag and Jack snatched it from her quickly.

'You'll need some 20ps for the launderette,' Caroline said, scrabbling around in her purse. Then she ripped a black rubbish sack from a roll and pushed it at Rebecca. 'You can put the washing in there.'

They sat in the launderette, eating the fish and chips greedily. They were alone apart from one woman, who kept giving them pitying glances, as if to say, 'what cruel parents, leaving their children to do the washing'. Jack stuck two chips up his nose and the woman turned away in disgust.

'Why does Caroline have to blame us for everything?' Jack asked. 'It's not fair.'

'It's only because of her china figure,' said Rebecca. 'If that hadn't got broken, she wouldn't be blaming us for this, would she? She doesn't trust us anymore.'

'What do you think she meant about Mum?' Jack asked. 'What can Mum've done?'

'I've got no idea,' said Rebecca. 'She might've done nothing and Caroline's just blaming her for it, like with us and the washing machine.'

As she watched the washing go round and round, a flurry of confused thoughts began to go round and round in her mind. She didn't want to think about Caroline, or about Mum. She tried to think of something else, and found her mind turning back to the china head. Wasn't it odd that wherever she'd put the head down, something happened?

There was the scratch on the bedside table, the hole in

the drawer, and now the washing machine breaking down. It was almost as if the thing was cursed.

'Knickers!' Jack shouted.

This was a new game that he'd invented, to embarrass her. It involved shouting 'knickers' every time he saw Rebecca's knickers in the washing machine window. The woman couldn't help glancing round, even though Rebecca could tell she was trying not to.

'Shut up, Jack!' Rebecca hissed.

But Jack was enjoying himself too much to stop.

'Knickers!' he cried out again.

Rebecca tried to distract him by telling him very quietly about her 'curse of the china head' theory.

'That's stupid,' Jack said when she'd finished. She had to admit it didn't sound at all believable when she said it out loud.

It was a huge relief when the washing was finally ready, although neither of them was looking forward to going back to Caroline's.

'We could knock on Charlie's door – I bet he'd let us stay,' Jack suggested.

'His place is tiny, there's no room. And anyway you can't go knocking on the door of someone you've only just met, and invite yourself to stay.'

'I wish we could,' Jack said miserably.

'I know.'

Caroline opened the door quickly this time.

'Your mum phoned while you were out,' she told them, in a 'by the way' kind of voice, as if it was nothing important.

'Mum?' Rebecca looked at her in dismay, her heart beating fast. It was unbelievable that Mum had phoned and they'd not been there. If only Caroline hadn't sent them to the launderette . . .

'What did she say?' Rebecca asked anxiously. 'Is she all right? Can we phone her back?'

'She didn't say much, but she said it's a bit awkward for you to phone her there. She'll try again later if she can.'

'Did you tell her about your ornament?' Jack wanted to know. 'And the flood?'

Caroline shook her head. 'Didn't see any point in worrying her now.'

'I wanted to speak to her,' Jack moaned, his face creasing up as if in pain.

'I'm sure she'll ring again,' Caroline said brusquely.

Rebecca waited all evening – listening for the phone to ring.

She cried herself to sleep.

Chapter 11

'What's the time, Becca? Can we go to Charlie's yet?'

Rebecca yawned, rubbed her eyes and looked at her little bedside clock. 'It's only six o'clock, Jack. Go back to bed.'

'I'm not tired.'

'Well, I am. Go and play in your room.'

'What with?'

'I don't know. Just go, will you.'

She heard herself snapping at him and felt bad, so she didn't protest when he pulled her curtain aside and said, 'I'll sit here and watch the sea. I won't make a sound, I promise.'

That'll be a first, she thought to herself, but she must have drifted back to sleep quickly. When she opened her eyes – she felt a strange sensation, as if someone was in the room. 'Jack,' she remembered with relief. She turned to the window. He wasn't there. She looked towards the door – and gasped.

What she saw sent a surge of terror right through her. Shadowy shapes were gliding into the room one by one.

What were they? *Ghosts*?

'It's a dream – it can only be a dream,' she told herself. She willed herself to wake up. But the shapes were still there. They were coming towards her, gathering round the bed – closing in on her. And now she could see more clearly. They weren't just shapes – they were figures, and there was something familiar about them.

One had a fancy red hat, another carried a fan. Rebecca had seen china figures like that in Caroline's ornament room. That's what they were! She suddenly realised – Caroline's china figures, swollen to full human size, floating just above the ground.

Rebecca's heart pounded. 'It's a dream, a dream, a silly dream,' she repeated over and over. 'I'm going to wake up any moment. Please – let me wake up.' She tried to move, to shake herself awake but it was as if her body was paralysed. She wanted to scream but no sound came.

Only the figures kept coming. They had no movement in their limbs; they looked as fragile as ever, but there was life in their swollen faces. There must have been fifteen of them round the bed – thirty demanding eyes staring into hers.

How had they got out? That had been the first fraught question in her dreaming mind. The room was locked. It must have been Jack. That was all she could think. He must have got hold of the key somehow and returned to the scene, like a criminal – unable to stay away.

The second question was – what did they want? That look in their eyes said they wanted something. That was for sure. It sent shivers right through her. Their faces seemed distorted, challenging her, cursing her. And where was Jack now? What had they done to him?

She woke in a sweat. It was half past eight. The dream felt so real that she looked round anxiously for Jack. He would be there now, she was sure. But he wasn't.

Rebecca panicked. She jumped out of bed, still half-asleep, and ran out onto the landing – unsure whether to check downstairs or up in Jack's room. His room was nearer – she'd try there first. Each foot on the stairs jerked her more awake. 'Calm down, it was only a dream,' she told herself. Even so she heaved a sigh of relief to see Jack lying on his bed, with his feet on the pillow, and bedding scattered everywhere. It was only when he looked up that she saw his face was red with tears. Her heart lurched.

'Jack! What's happened?'

'Nothing,' Jack mumbled, sniffing and rubbing his eyes. 'I want Mum, that's all. I miss her, Becca.'

'Oh, Jack.' Rebecca sat on the bed and hugged him, making soothing noises, for her own benefit as much as his. Her heart was still thudding from the dream.

'Geroff me, I'm all right,' said Jack, pulling away and sitting up. 'Can we go to Charlie's now?'

Downstairs, they found that Caroline had already made their packed lunches. She hurried them through breakfast, as if she was certain they'd break something else at any minute.

'I'll see you later then,' she said, as she swept them out of the front door.

'What if Mum phones?' Rebecca asked, just before the door closed.

'Don't worry, I'll tell her to ring back this evening,' said Caroline, and the door clicked shut.

As they walked down the road towards the antique shop, images from the dream kept flashing through Rebecca's mind. She walked faster, as if trying to shake them off.

Jack speeded up and overtook her, clearly determined to be the first to reach Charlie. Rebecca wasn't bothered about Charlie, but she did want to know what his dad had found out about the china figure. She caught Jack up as he reached the shop. They could see Charlie through the window, talking to his dad.

'Hi, Charlie!' called Jack.

'Hiya,' said Charlie, as they walked in. He reached out just in time to catch a white jug that Jack had knocked with his elbow.

'Jack!' Rebecca said crossly.

'I didn't touch it,' said Jack.

Rebecca raised her eyebrows. Charlie grinned.

'Now,' said Charlie's dad. 'As you've made friends with my son here, I think I should introduce myself. Ray Matthews, at your service. You can call me Ray.'

Rebecca winced at the word 'friends'. Hanging about with Charlie the day before didn't make him a *friend* as far she was concerned.

'Right,' said Ray. 'You'll be wanting to know what I've found out about your figurine. Where did I put that head?'

As he reached up to a shelf behind him Rebecca noticed that he had a white bandage wrapped round his hand. It certainly hadn't been there the day before.

'What happened to your hand?' she asked, staring at it.

'He burnt it on the cooker,' Charlie explained.

Rebecca felt her own hand flinch in sympathy, and then she remembered her last sighting of the china head – sitting in the centre of Ray's open right hand.

'Clumsy oaf, aren't you, Dad?' Charlie teased.

Ray shook his head. 'Cooker's old, you see,' he explained. 'Get's overheated, that's all – nothing to do with clumsiness. Looks like this shelf needs replacing too – see this crack, Charlie. I've never noticed that before.'

Charlie moved closer and ran his finger along the crack, which was too high for Rebecca or Jack to see.

Rebecca's mind was whirring giddily as Ray took down the china head. Everyone else was acting as if nothing particular had happened – even Jack clearly hadn't remembered what she'd said in the launderette.

'Are you okay?' Charlie asked her. 'You look like you've seen a ghost.'

'I'm fine,' she managed to murmur, but the string of events was racing through her mind like a train through a dark tunnel. The pain in her hand, the bedside table, the drawer, the washing machine – and now Ray's hand and the antique shop shelf… Everywhere the china head had spent any length of time – something had happened. Too many times to be coincidence. But what did it all mean?

Chapter 12

Ray spoke solemnly. 'I've bad news for you, I'm afraid.'

Rebecca thought for a moment he was going to say, 'This head is cursed,' but what he did say was almost as horrific.

'You're talking five to seven hundred pounds to replace one of these.'

Rebecca gasped. 'That much?'

'It's a rare piece, only produced from 1931–38, so you're not likely to find one, anyway. It's quite something to hold one of these – even if it is just the head.' Ray smiled down at the head in his hand and then held it out to her. She didn't want to take it. 'Here – you might as well have it back. I've no use for it.'

Reluctantly, she took it with her fingertips, dropping it quickly into their packed lunch bag as if it was red-hot. Ray's words were beginning to sink in, and they filled her with despair. She didn't know why – but replacing the figurine felt so important now, like it was the only way to make things better.

Charlie looked at her and then back at Ray. 'You've found some rare pieces before, Dad, haven't you?' he said. 'Couldn't you at least try to find one? I remember that teacup you found for that old lady who'd broken one of a set. You said it would be impossible – but you found one, didn't you?'

Ray turned to Charlie. 'Once in a blue moon, these things happen, son. But that figure – no chance, I'm telling you straight.'

'I bet I could find one,' Charlie challenged.

'We couldn't pay for it anyway,' Rebecca muttered, shaking her head. 'So there's no point looking.'

Ray smiled. 'If you find a figurine in that series I'll pay for it myself. That's how rare they are.'

'I'll hold you to that, Dad.' Charlie grinned. 'Here – write down the number and the series so I can look out for one.'

'Charlie,' said Jack, 'can we play on your computer again?'

'Maybe later. I need to get out of this place for a bit.'

Rebecca felt relieved. The last thing she wanted was a morning stuck in Charlie's room. But her relief was short-lived.

'Do you want me to show you the sights?' Charlie asked. 'There's the lighthouse, and there's Gun Hill with all the cannons, the river and the ferry...'

'We haven't seen any of that, have we, Becca?' said Jack.

Rebecca shook her head. 'Are you sure you've got nothing better to do?' she asked Charlie.

He grinned. 'You're in luck. The Charlie Matthews guided tour starts right here! This way if you please! And do try to keep up. I don't want any stragglers!'

Rebecca wished she could tell him they had other plans, but they didn't. At least it would keep Jack occupied.

She turned to Ray. 'I'm sorry we wasted your time,

and I'm sorry about your hand. I hope it gets better soon.'

'This?' Ray held up his bandaged hand. 'Don't you go worrying about this. Tough as old boots, I am. And it was no bother at all – I only wish I could give you better news. Best get some flowers for your aunt instead, eh?'

'Yeh, Becca – we'll get her some flowers. That'll sort her,' said Jack.

As they set off down the road, Rebecca wondered what to do about the china head. The dream was still bothering her too. It had been a dream, hadn't it? The reality itself seemed so unbelievable, she couldn't get things straight in her mind. The blue plastic bag felt increasingly heavy in her hand.

'We'll find one of those figurines, don't you worry,' Charlie said confidently.

'Like where?' Rebecca asked.

'Antiques fairs, car boot sales, auctions, house clearance – I love hunting for things at these places. Usually it's cars I'm after, like I showed you, but I don't mind what it is – it's the search that's fun.'

Rebecca shrugged. 'Your dad says they're rare. He must know what he's talking about.'

'But he said he'd even pay for it if we found one. I can't resist a challenge like that. What have we got to lose?'

'You coming?' Jack had run ahead and was calling them. 'Which way now?'

'Left,' Charlie shouted. He turned back to Rebecca. 'There's an antiques fair in Halesworth on Sunday. I was going anyway, but you two can come if you like. The more eyes to look, the better. You can bring that head so we make sure we know what we're looking for.'

'Maybe.' Rebecca didn't want to commit herself. She imagined the destruction Jack could cause at a whole fair full of antiques.

Charlie took them to see the lighthouse first, which looked odd as it was on the street, among the houses and not out on a cliff edge. Charlie said they'd built it there because two old lighthouses on a cliff further down the coast had been washed into the sea when the cliffs eroded.

Jack lost interest in the lighthouse once he found out they couldn't go inside and climb up it.

'I'll take you to Gun Hill,' Charlie told him. 'You can climb on the cannons.'

Gun Hill turned out to be a patch of grass overlooking the sea, with six huge iron cannons mounted on concrete with wooden surrounds and iron wheels. The wood was cut in steps so they were easy to climb up.

Jack was in his element, climbing up and sitting astride each cannon in turn, making loud gunfire noises.

'Keep it down, Jack,' Rebecca begged.

Jack called down to Charlie. 'These are wicked. Do they really work? Why are they here?'

He was full of questions that Charlie clearly couldn't answer. 'I don't know much about them,' he told Jack. 'You should ask your aunt – she's supposed to be into history and all that, isn't she?'

Jack made a face.

They had lunch at Charlie's, and spent the afternoon with him as well. On the way back to Caroline's they stopped to buy some flowers with the money left over from the fish and chips.

'Which ones do you think she'll like?' Rebecca asked anxiously.

Jack shrugged and pointed to some yellow chrysanthemums. 'Those, I reckon.'

They were bright and cheerful, and not too much money, so Rebecca bought them.

'These are for you,' she told Caroline when she opened the door to them. Caroline looked at the flowers in surprise.

'It's to say sorry,' Rebecca explained, 'for the china lady.'

Caroline said nothing and Rebecca found herself babbling. 'We are sorry about the figurine – but the washing machine really wasn't our fault, I promise you.'

Caroline took the flowers, but seemed undecided about what to say. She opened her mouth, but at that moment the phone rang and she hurried off to answer it.

'It's your mother,' she called.

'Me first! I want to talk to her first!' Jack cried, charging down the hallway.

Rebecca waited impatiently while Jack jabbered on about the cannons.

'How are you, Mum?' she asked, when she finally managed to prise the phone away from Jack.

Mum sounded distant and more subdued than Rebecca had hoped. 'I'm doing okay.' She sighed. 'But how about you – I've been so worried. Is Jack behaving himself? Is Caroline treating you all right?'

'Yes,' Rebecca lied. 'We're both fine. Caroline's been very kind. Is it okay there?'

'It's hard, love. Some people have already given up

and gone off – they couldn't handle it, you see. But I'm going to do it. I think about you two and that makes me determined. However hard it is – I'm going to do it. Look I have to go now, we've got this group therapy session in a minute. Love you lots.'

Rebecca only just had time to say, 'Love you too, Mum,' before the phone clicked.

She felt the disappointment in the pit of her stomach. She had been looking forward so much to speaking to Mum and now it was over. Mum hadn't said if or when she'd be able to phone again. Rebecca had wanted reassurance but she didn't feel reassured. It wasn't what Mum had said, exactly. It was the shaky note in her voice. Mum had never seemed very strong. If other people had already given up, how was Mum going to make it?

Chapter 13

When they sat down to eat, Caroline thanked them briefly for the flowers, which she had put in a vase on the table. She didn't smile. Rebecca wished they hadn't bought them. Poxy flowers couldn't make up for a precious ornament, could they?

'Can I ask you something?' Jack said to Caroline.

Rebecca held her breath. She wasn't sure if now was the right time for him to start asking about the photos.

Caroline looked at him uncertainly. 'What do you want to ask?'

'It's about the cannons – you know on that hill – Gun Hill, is it? Why are they there? Are they real – I mean do they work? Charlie said I should ask you because you know about history and everything.'

'Charlie?' Caroline asked. 'Is that Ray Matthews's son? How did you meet him?'

'In the arcade,' said Jack. 'We just got talking and he said he'd show us the sights.'

'He did, did he? Well, I hope you haven't been spending all my money in the arcade.'

'No,' Rebecca assured her.

'We were only looking,' Jack lied.

Rebecca gritted her teeth as she met his eyes.

'Well, I can certainly tell you about the cannons.'

Rebecca was surprised to catch a glimpse of a smile from Caroline.

'Let's clear up from supper first and then we can sit down in the lounge.'

As they cleared the table, Rebecca braced herself for a history lecture. Jack was bound to lose interest after the first few seconds and it would all be a big embarrassment. She excused herself to go to the toilet and found her mind returning to the china head. She had left it, still in the plastic bag, on the floor of her room. Nothing else had happened. Maybe, however unlikely it sounded, all the strange things had been coincidences.

When she returned, Caroline was already well under way in the lounge. She looked different somehow – her brow less creased, her eyes sparkling and her hands gesturing enthusiastically as she spoke. Jack was leaning forward, listening.

'Did you hear that, Becca? They *are* real cannons and they're old ones. They had wars here in the old days – big ships out at sea and everything. You wouldn't think that, would you? One soldier was even killed when a cannon backfired!'

Rebecca sat down and listened as Caroline continued. She told them how the town was bombarded in the 1914–18 war because the Germans thought it was fortified due to the cannons on the cliff; how they were taken down and buried during the Second World War to prevent the same thing happening.

Rebecca found it hard to imagine the place as a battle zone. It was such a peaceful holiday resort now. She looked up at Caroline, who seemed so cheerful that Rebecca began to wonder if the flowers *had* done the trick. Maybe Caroline had forgiven them and everything was going to be okay. She and Jack listened eagerly and Caroline looked pleased that her history lesson had been a success.

'Can I ask you something else?' said Jack.

'Yes, go on.' Caroline was clearly enjoying herself.

'Why did you and Mum never talk for all those years?'

Rebecca saw Caroline's expression change dramatically. It was as if her face closed up and her eyes and mouth withdrew inside her head. The colour in her face disappeared and the cold, hard look returned.

'That,' she said stiffly, 'is none of your business. Now I think it's time you both went to bed.'

Rebecca gave Jack a furious look.

'I was only asking,' he said. 'You did say I could ask . . .'

'To bed, now!'

'Why did you have to start asking that?' Rebecca moaned to Jack, as they made their way upstairs, 'and just when she was being a bit friendlier.'

'That's why I asked her, you nithead. I thought as she was in a good mood she might tell us.'

'Well you were wrong.'

Jack shrugged.

'I'm going to have a bath,' Rebecca told him. 'You'd better go and get changed.'

Rebecca lazed in the bath for a long time. When she came out of the bathroom, she found Jack in his pyjama bottoms on her bedroom floor. He had his knees up and was balancing something on his head and letting it drop onto his knee. As it rolled off his leg, she realised with horror that it was the china head.

'What are you doing?' she demanded. She grabbed the head and thrust it back in the bag.

'Messing about, that's all. Keep your hair on!'

Rebecca looked at him anxiously. She should have talked to him earlier – after the antique shop, so he knew the risk and didn't touch the head.

'Don't you remember what I said to you yesterday – in the launderette?'

'Stop shouting "knickers"?'

'No, not that, you idiot. About the head – all the strange things that have happened – wherever it's been. The scratch on that table, the hole in the drawer – look – here.' She pulled out the drawer and held it up to show him. 'Then the washing machine – and I'd forgotten about my hand. Don't you remember how my hand hurt – and it was the hand I'd been holding that head in the day before. And now this morning – Charlie's dad, Ray – he'd hurt his hand too – and there was a crack on the shelf where he'd put the head. Don't you see – it's too many things . . . '

Jack looked thoughtful. 'But, Becca, it's only a broken piece of ornament – that's all. How can it do things like that?'

'I don't know, do I? But there's something weird about it, isn't there? I know it sounds crazy but I feel like it wants revenge – for having been broken. How long have you been playing with it?'

'I dunno. Since you got in the bath. I was only messing about.'

He was looking worried now and she began to wish

she hadn't said anything. She'd only frightened him – and it wasn't as if they could do anything about it now.

'I held it too, remember,' said Jack, 'when I got it off the washing machine. Nothing's happened to *my* hand.'

'Yes,' Rebecca admitted. 'But you only held it for a second. I think it has to be somewhere for longer than that before it does anything.'

'It's been in that bag all day and nothing's happened, has it?' Jack said hopefully.

'I know,' Rebecca admitted, examining the bag. 'I think it's okay in the bag. I don't know why. Maybe it doesn't work on plastic.'

'Nothing's gonna happen to me,' Jack said with determination.

'You're probably right,' she told him, wishing she believed it.

Chapter 14

Jack was fine in the morning.

'See,' he told Rebecca. 'You were just trying to scare me, weren't you? Well, it didn't work.'

Rebecca was glad – but still anxious. At breakfast she nibbled half-heartedly at a piece of toast, while Jack tucked in to some scrambled eggs.

'Aren't you hungry?' asked Caroline.

Rebecca shook her head. She couldn't eat – not with so much on her mind.

Caroline made packed lunches and they set off to meet Charlie again. Rebecca still wasn't sure about him but she had to admit that he seemed more able to keep Jack happy than she was. She even felt a little jealous.

The shop wasn't open yet so they went round the side. From the way Charlie looked at her when he opened the door, Rebecca sensed that the worry she was feeling must have shown on her face.

'Cheer up,' said Charlie, bending his head on one side. 'Can't be that bad, can it?'

'Fat lot you know about it,' she retorted.

'Sorry, sorry.' Charlie looked startled by her hostility towards him. He turned to Jack. 'What's up with her?'

Jack shrugged. 'What are we going to do today, Charlie?'

'How about I show you the river and the ferry?' said

Charlie. He looked warily at Rebecca, as if unsure how she was going to react.

'We can, can't we, Becca?' said Jack.

Rebecca hesitated. What if Jack fell in? What if he drowned? But Jack was already getting excited with Charlie and she didn't want to be a spoilsport.

'All right,' she said.

They began to walk.

'How's your dad's hand?' Rebecca asked.

'Oh, it's better today,' said Charlie. 'I know he's got that bandage on it but it's only a little burn. Big fuss about nothing – that's Dad. It's no big deal.'

'Becca thinks . . . ' Jack began but she gave him a dig in the ribs and he shut up.

'Thinks what?' Charlie asked, turning to Rebecca.

'It must have been painful – a burn like that,' she said, thinking quickly.

'Forget about it,' said Charlie. 'Look – here we are.'

They had reached the river. Rebecca had expected it to be wide because Charlie had talked about the ferry. She had pictured a big cross-channel type ferry that cars drove onto. This river was only about two ferries wide.

It was pretty though, with the water lapping softly against the banks and little jetties all along. Small boats nudged each other as if they were sharing secrets. There was a strong smell of fish.

Jack climbed up a stack of wooden logs, leapt off and began kicking at a twisted pile of ropes and nets on the ground. Then he walked out onto a jetty that had a clear sign saying 'Private, Keep Off'.

'Jack – get off there!' Rebecca called. He ignored her

as usual. She wished she'd put her foot down about the river. It was a crazy place to bring someone like Jack – and after last night... Rebecca pushed the china head from her mind.

'Over here, Jack,' Charlie beckoned. 'I'll show you the ferry.'

Jack came running towards them. 'Where is it?'

'This way.' Charlie led them along the grassy river's edge path. Rebecca could see hazards everywhere for Jack. If he ran and slipped he might crash against a boat or jetty, or get caught in a motor.

'Be careful, Jack,' she couldn't help saying.

He tutted and raised his eyebrows, then deliberately stepped even closer to the water's edge.

'This is it,' said Charlie, stopping where four people were hovering on the bank.

Rebecca was stunned to see a small wooden rowing boat approaching the jetty.

'That?' said Jack. 'That's not a ferry.'

'It is round here,' said Charlie. 'Danni, the ferry-woman there – her dad rowed it before her. It's been going for years.'

'Can we go on it, Becca?' Jack begged. 'I love boats and we never get to go on one.'

Rebecca could see people holding money out to the ferryman. 'What does it cost?' she asked Charlie. 'We're a bit short...' They had run out of money completely, though she didn't like to admit it.

'It's only 50p and I'll pay anyway,' said Charlie.

'Come on,' said Jack, as if the decision was made. Rebecca hesitated.

'Wait, Jack,' she called. She turned to Charlie. 'I'll pay you back once I have the money.'

'It's no big deal,' said Charlie.

As she looked towards the river Rebecca saw with horror that Jack was about to bypass the queue and leap off the jetty into the ferry. She opened her mouth to yell at him but luckily the ferrywoman saw him and was quick-witted enough to grab hold of him.

Rebecca ran to them. 'Sorry,' she said to the ferrywoman and turned furiously to Jack. 'Jack – you have to wait your turn like everyone else.'

'I wasn't doing anything,' said Jack.

Rebecca sighed. 'You're showing off to Charlie – that's what you're doing. Just give us a break, will you?'

Charlie joined them. 'Okay?' he asked.

'Fine,' Rebecca said, in a not-fine voice.

When they were at last all sitting down in the ferry, the ferrywoman began rowing them rhythmically out into the centre of the river. Jack sat back, letting his fingers dangle in the water. At last he seemed a bit calmer. Rebecca relaxed a little, listening to the gentle slap slap of the water against the boat. She actually began to enjoy the experience.

'I love this river,' said Charlie.

For once Rebecca couldn't help agreeing with him.

'What's on the other side?' Jack asked.

'Walberswick,' said Charlie. 'It's a small village.'

Jack made a face. 'Is that all? Can't we stay on the ferry and keep going across the river and back again. I don't want to go to a boring village.'

Rebecca wouldn't have minded staying on the ferry

all day herself.

As they approached the bank, her nerves began to tingle once more. She wished Jack had a bit more sense of danger – a bit more sense altogether.

'Here, I'll get out first and give you a hand up,' Charlie told Jack.

Rebecca knew if she'd suggested that, Jack would have insisted he didn't need help. Yet he was perfectly happy to be helped by Charlie.

With Jack safely ashore, Charlie turned and held his hand out to Rebecca. She took it reluctantly, letting go as soon as she had stepped onto the jetty.

'Jack! Wait for us!' she called – as she saw that Jack was already busy exploring the riverbank.

'Don't go near those reeds!' Charlie warned Jack. 'You can't see where the land ends and the water begins. We'd never get you out if you fell in there.'

Jack looked at Charlie doubtfully while Rebecca's heart skipped a beat.

'We'll go this way,' Charlie told Jack, indicating a narrow road that led away from the river through a small car park. Jack bounded ahead.

Charlie turned to Rebecca. 'Jeez, you must get exhausted having to watch him like this all the time. He's wearing me out already.'

'He's my brother – I don't have much choice,' Rebecca pointed out. She looked ahead in search of Jack and was just in time to see him running straight into the path of an oncoming car.

'Jack!' Rebecca shrieked, as the car screeched to a halt, missing him by inches.

Jack rushed on oblivious.

Rebecca ran to catch him up. 'Jack – come back and walk with us – you'll get yourself killed.'

'Stop fussing – I'm fine,' said Jack. He gave her a sideways stare. 'You think that china head's going to make something happen to me, don't you? I thought you were teasing me but you really believe it, don't you?'

'Of course not,' Rebecca said sharply. 'If you carry on behaving like this you'll kill yourself with no help from anyone.'

'What's that about the china head?' asked Charlie, who was closer behind than Rebecca had realised.

'Oh,' Rebecca stuttered, 'just that, err, we would like to come to that antiques fair with you at the weekend if it's still okay. If there's any chance of finding a figurine like that one for Caroline, it has to be worth a try.'

Charlie grinned.

He treated them to ice-creams – which meant owing him more money. Then he took them to Walberswick beach – which to Rebecca's relief, seemed a lot safer than the river. Charlie bought himself a sandwich and they ate their packed lunches. Rebecca lay sunbathing while Jack and Charlie paddled and competed to see who could throw a pebble the furthest out to sea. It was after four when they made their way back to the river.

'What're they doing?' Jack asked, pointing to some boys who were sitting on a bridge that went over a small creek.

'Crabbing, I should think,' said Charlie.

'Catch crabs?' Jack exclaimed. 'What – and then eat them? Yuck!'

'I wouldn't want to do that – it's cruel,' Rebecca agreed.

'They're not for eating,' said Charlie. 'You just catch them and see who can catch the biggest. You keep them in a bucket of water – then when you've finished you put them back in the river.'

'Can we have a go?' asked Jack.

'Another time,' said Charlie. 'I've got all the gear at home. There's a Crabbing Championship here next week. We can go in for it if you like – if you're still here, that is.'

He led them back to the ferry jetty where there was a long queue. They stood in line and watched the ferry going back and forth until it was finally their turn.

'Don't do anything stupid,' Rebecca warned Jack.

To her relief, they made it safe and sound back to the Southwold side.

They walked on into the town and then said their goodbyes. Charlie headed off speedily towards the antique shop.

'I don't want to go back to Caroline's yet,' moaned Jack.

'Well I'm tired out,' said Rebecca.

As they walked, Rebecca wondered what kind of mood Caroline would be in. If only Jack hadn't asked about her and Mum. It must have been something awful that happened between them.

She turned to speak to Jack, and realised he wasn't beside her.

'Yoo hoo! Up here!' came Jack's voice.

She looked up to see that he was balancing, arms

outstretched, on a narrow brick wall, that was well over two metres high.

'Get down,' she said firmly, but Jack began to walk even faster along the wall.

'I'm fine,' he told her.

Then she saw his foot slip. His arms floundered in the air. He looked like he was going to come flying down onto the pavement. She reached up to try and break his fall, but to her relief he regained his balance. He smirked. 'You thought I was gonna fall, didn't you?'

'Get down from there *now*!' Rebecca demanded. But Jack defiantly continued along the wall.

Then it happened. He wobbled and swayed towards her. He tried to swing himself back the other way. But this time he must have swung too far.

'Jack!' she yelled, as first one foot and then the other slipped off the wall. She heard him cry out as he disappeared behind it. She heard a thud. Then nothing.

Chapter 15

'Jack!' Rebecca screamed. 'Jack!'

He didn't answer. She looked wildly around. There was no one in sight. She clutched at the wall and tried to find a foothold. Her sandals wouldn't grip. She knew there was no way she could climb up, even if she took them off. It was too high. Instead she began to run alongside the wall. There must be a way through somewhere. But the wall seemed to go on and on.

'Jack!' she screamed again. There was a gate – she'd found a gate. She pulled at it. It didn't open. Was it locked? No – there was a catch, and her hands were shaking too much to work it. She tried to calm herself. She was through. She charged down the brick path that ran beside a flowerbed along the wall.

'Jack!' she yelled piercingly, as he came into sight. He was lying awkwardly across the path – still, too still. Jack was never that still.

She bent over him – helpless, panicking and trying to remember how to tell if someone was alive. A pulse – that was it. Did he have a pulse? She lifted his hand. It was terrifyingly limp. She held his wrist but she couldn't find a pulse. Then she remembered – the neck, it was easier to find a pulse at the neck. She tried. She thought she could feel a pulse – or was it her own?

She felt tears welling up. 'Jack! Wake up!'

She wanted to shake him but feared she might do him more harm – if he was alive, that was.

She had a sudden flashback to Mum on the sofa at home – only weeks ago, though it seemed like a lifetime. She had come home and found her – so still, so pale. She hadn't known if Mum was out of it or dead. She couldn't wake her. The same panic. The same panic as this. But then she'd reached for the phone – called for an ambulance. She needed a phone now. She needed help.

Rebecca looked around frantically. She had been vaguely aware of a house as she'd rushed through the gate. She turned to it now. It was a big house that stood imposingly within the wall and gardens. She ran to the front door and banged on it desperately. No one came. She banged again. The house had a deserted feel to it. The curtains of the downstairs rooms were drawn.

She had no option but to run back to the gate. 'I'll be back,' she called to Jack. 'I'm going for help.'

Giddy and breathless she charged through the gate and straight into a passing woman.

'Watch where you're . . . ' The woman saw the state Rebecca was in and changed her tone. 'Are you all right, dear?'

'No – it's my brother, he's fallen off that wall. I need an ambulance – I think he's dead!' she cried.

The woman pulled a mobile phone from her bag and quickly pressed 999. 'Where exactly is he?' and 'What's his name?' she asked Rebecca, who managed to mumble the answers between sobs.

'Take me to him,' the woman said, putting the phone back in her bag. 'The ambulance will be here soon.'

Rebecca ran and the woman ran with her until they reached Jack, who was lying as still and white as he'd been when she left him.

'He's dead, isn't he?' Rebecca sobbed, as the woman bent over Jack.

'No, no, he's not dead,' the woman assured her, as she examined him. 'He has a pulse and he's breathing – he's just in a kind of faint.'

Rebecca rubbed her eyes. The woman was pulling off her cardigan. She laid it across Jack's shoulders.

'That'll keep him warm until the ambulance arrives,' she said, and she put an arm round Rebecca.

At that moment Rebecca saw Jack's hand twitch. Then his eyes opened. He winced and tried to move. 'Mum! Mum!' he moaned.

'Jack!' Rebecca could do nothing but say his name; she was overwhelmed with relief to hear his voice.

'It's all right, love, you've had a nasty fall,' the woman told Jack. 'Just keep still now. An ambulance is coming soon to take you to hospital.'

Jack closed his eyes.

'Where are your parents?' the woman asked Rebecca.

'*Where are your parents? Where are your parents?*' The dreaded question seemed to echo all around.

'They're not here,' Rebecca said finally. 'We're staying with our aunt, Caroline Walters – do you know her?'

'No, love, I'm only here on holiday. Here – use my phone and give her a ring.'

Rebecca took the phone gratefully, but then stared at it.

'I don't know the number,' she told the woman. 'She only lives two turnings away – should I go and get her?'

'Tell me where and I'll go for you,' said the woman. 'You'd better stay here with your brother until the ambulance comes.'

Rebecca didn't want to be left but she didn't fancy breaking the news to Caroline either.

'Thank you,' she said, giving her the address and directions.

Once she'd gone, Rebecca sat on the path beside Jack and waited.

She wished Mum was here.

The ambulance man and woman seemed to appear from nowhere. The man asked Rebecca lots of questions while the woman examined Jack.

'Will he be okay?' Rebecca asked.

'Looks to me like a touch of concussion, and I'm not sure about that leg,' the ambulance-woman explained. 'We'll know more once we've got him to the hospital. Now, where are your...'

But she didn't get to the 'parents' bit, for at that moment Caroline appeared.

'Are you their mother?' the ambulance-man asked Caroline.

'No, no – I'm their aunt,' Caroline panted. 'I'm responsible for them – what's happened to Jack?'

Rebecca saw that her face was full of concern. Was it real concern, or was she only worried about what Mum would think when she heard? Rebecca couldn't tell.

Jack came round again in the ambulance and started screaming. Then he was sick. Rebecca began to worry once more that he was going to die. She squeezed his hand.

'We'll have to phone Mum,' she said to Caroline. 'She'll want to be here, won't she?'

Caroline hesitated before answering. 'Let's see how serious it is, first.' She lowered her voice as she continued. 'Your mother has enough to worry about. If she comes out of the clinic early, it might be very hard to get her to go back there. Then the treatment might not work. I don't think we should tell her unless it's absolutely necessary. Do you see what I'm getting at?'

'I suppose,' said Rebecca. 'But if it's bad you will tell her, won't you?'

'Of course,' said Caroline. She reached out an arm and put it awkwardly on Rebecca's shoulder.

Chapter 16

The waiting around at the hospital was a blur of swishing white coats and unintelligible voices. It turned out that Jack had hit his head and badly bruised his left leg when he fell. They decided he should stay in overnight so they could keep an eye on his concussion.

Jack was admitted to the children's ward and the nurse gave him some painkillers, which she said would make him sleepy. Caroline left Rebecca by his bed and went off to have another word with the doctor.

'I want Mum,' Jack whimpered, once they were alone.

Rebecca looked at him uneasily. She wanted Mum too, more than anything. 'If she hears what's happened she'll be straight here,' said Rebecca, 'you know she will – but... listen, Jack, Caroline doesn't think we should tell her.'

'Why?' Jack demanded.

'It's just that... if she comes, then she might not go back in the clinic – she might not get off the drugs and it might be how it was before. You don't want that, do you?'

'No,' Jack sobbed, 'but I want Mum.'

'You've got to be brave,' said Rebecca. 'It'll be no good if she comes now.'

'Don't leave me here, Becca,' Jack begged.

'I have to. I can't stay. You'll go to sleep and when

you wake up tomorrow we'll be here – I'll make sure Caroline gets up early and brings me. Then if everything's okay the doctor says you can come back with us in the morning.'

'I don't want to go to Caroline's – I want to go home.'

'Oh, Jack.' Rebecca squeezed his hand tight. Jack closed his eyes.

Caroline came back at that moment. 'The nurses will look after you,' she told Jack, 'and we'll be back first thing in the morning.' She leant over him, but he was already asleep.

She turned to Rebecca. 'Come on, we'll let him rest.'

Rebecca hesitated. What if he woke up in the night? Who would comfort him?

'We can ring the hospital later and check that he's okay,' said Caroline, holding the ward door for Rebecca.

Rebecca took one last look at the sleeping Jack and followed Caroline out of the ward.

They took a cab back to Caroline's. As soon as the hospital was out of sight, Rebecca began to cry.

'I'm sorry,' she sobbed, 'really I am. I should've stopped him climbing on that wall – I did try you know. I tried to stop him. He wouldn't come down.'

'No,' Caroline said firmly, meeting Rebecca's weepy eyes with a serious expression. 'It's not your fault. I should never have left you to look after him on your own. It was selfish and thoughtless of me.' She shook her head as if in dismay at her own behaviour. Then she sighed. 'There are reasons, reasons you wouldn't understand. You don't know how hard it was for me to let you come here – Stephanie's children. If you knew...'

'Well, tell me then,' Rebecca blurted out. 'Tell me!'

Caroline shook her head. 'It wouldn't be fair.'

'It's not fair keeping us in the dark,' Rebecca exclaimed. She felt a surge of fury with Caroline. 'Anyway – why did you say you'd have us if you didn't want us here? I was so scared of us going into care – but anything would have been better than being here with you. You don't care at all. You care more about your precious ornaments than you do about your own family!'

There was a long silence. Finally Caroline spoke. 'That's not true. In the circumstances it was very generous of me to take you in at all. You know your mother and I hadn't talked for years. And then she rings up, out of the blue and starts asking favours – and no small ones at that.'

'I know – but why did you and Mum stop talking?' Rebecca demanded. 'Jack's a nightmare sometimes, the way he behaves, but he's my brother, he always will be. I love him. Nothing would make me stop talking to him, whatever he did.'

'I'd have said that about your mother too,' Caroline said wistfully, 'before it happened.'

'Before what happened?'

'When you're older,' said Caroline.

'I want to know now,' Rebecca insisted.

Caroline was silent. The taxi came to a halt.

Inside the house Caroline made them both a sweet milky tea. It was half past ten. They'd been at the hospital for hours.

'I was a little younger than you when your mother

was born,' Caroline began. She had a dreamy look in her eyes.

She's going to tell me, thought Rebecca, trying to wake herself up more. She said she wouldn't but now she's going to! She sat up and gave Caroline her full attention.

Caroline sipped her tea and continued. 'She was a surprise to our parents – they didn't think they could have any more children. By the time Steph was born, Dad was ill and Mum was trying to run this place as a guesthouse, look after Dad and the new baby – so of course, I had to do what I could to help. I spent a lot of time looking after your mother when she was young. What with that and studying, I never had time for much of a social life.'

'It wasn't *her* fault,' Rebecca commented. 'You didn't stop talking to Mum because of that, did you?'

'No, no. Of course not. We were close back then, although she always was a bit wild. We had to be on our best behaviour here with guests staying all the time. Your mother hated that.' Caroline paused.

'Go on,' said Rebecca.

'Well – it's just that I know how hard it was for me – having to look after her. So I shouldn't have left you on your own to take care of Jack, especially with the way he behaves, and everything you must have been through with your mother. I should think you've been looking after her a fair bit, as well as Jack. That's not how things should be. I lost part of my childhood looking after Steph – you shouldn't lose yours watching over Jack. It's us adults who should be responsible.'

'Tell me more,' Rebecca begged. 'Please – tell me what happened with you and Mum, why you fell out.'

Caroline sat up sharply and looked at her watch. 'It's after eleven,' she said standing up. 'You'd better get to bed if we're going to have an early start. I'll just ring the hospital to check on Jack.'

'I want to know – please.'

Caroline met her eyes. Her face was serious and full of pain. 'You don't. You don't want to know. I promise you.'

'But...'

Caroline stood up and headed down the hallway to the phone.

Rebecca protested, but it was no use. She was clearly not going to prise any more information out of Caroline that night. She waited while Caroline made the phone call to the hospital and was relieved to hear that Jack was sleeping peacefully. Then she made her way up to bed.

As she entered the bedroom she glanced down at the plastic bag containing the china head. It lay on the floor in the corner, where they'd left it after Jack had been playing with it the previous evening. Rebecca looked at it warily. She didn't want it in the room with her, but she certainly wasn't going to touch it.

She slept fitfully, waking frequently so that the night seemed to go on forever. Finally, when she woke, light was peeking through the curtains and her watch said it was half past seven. She got up and went to the toilet. She couldn't hear any sounds that might suggest Caroline was up.

Coming back into the bedroom she found herself looking down once more at the bag containing the china head. She realised uneasily that however hard she'd tried to convince herself that the head couldn't be responsible for the things that had happened, a nagging voice inside her was telling her it was true. She must do something about it, she decided. She would throw the head away. That would stop the strange things happening, once and for all.

Without giving herself a chance for second thoughts, she took the bag straight down to the kitchen and pushed it deep into the bin.

Chapter 17

In the car on the way to fetch Jack from the hospital, Rebecca tried once more to prise information out of Caroline.

'Please – tell me about you and Mum,' she begged.

'Right now we have to think about Jack,' said Caroline, ignoring Rebecca's pleas. 'If they let him out, I expect he'll have to rest indoors for a few days.'

'He's going to be a nightmare,' said Rebecca. 'Jack can't stand keeping still at the best of times. What's he going to do if he can't go out?'

She pictured the scene. Caroline would want to get on with her work, and she'd be left to keep Jack occupied somehow. It was going to be hell.

'I'll look after him,' said Caroline. 'You can have a bit of time to yourself.'

Rebecca looked at her in surprise. 'I don't mind staying with him . . . I mean – you don't know how he is . . . '

'He'll be fine with me,' Caroline insisted.

Rebecca was less sure. She yearned for some time to herself, but how could she go off and leave Jack with Caroline? Jack would hate it – he'd be furious.

When they reached Jack's ward he looked delighted to see them (well, Rebecca, anyway) and had a much better colour than the previous day.

'At last!' he said. 'I saw that doctor – he says I can

go. Becca, look at my bruise – it's black and yellow *and* green!'

Rebecca looked. The bruising was impressive.

'Does it hurt?' she asked.

'Not much. I've still got a headache though. Come on – get me out of here, I hate this place.'

'I'll need to speak to the nurse, maybe the doctor too,' said Caroline. 'You wait here with him, Rebecca.'

Caroline hurried off.

'Did you sleep okay?' Rebecca asked Jack. She was wondering how she was going to break the news that Caroline wanted to look after him.

'I did till that boy started puking everywhere,' said Jack, pointing to a mound in the opposite bed, which looked as if it was now sleeping soundly. 'It was disgusting.'

'Why did you do it?' Rebecca suddenly demanded. 'What made you climb on that wall? You could've died!'

Jack frowned. 'I don't remember a thing – honest, Becca. All I know is, I was walking with you and then I woke up on the ground. I didn't even know where I was. It must've been that china head that made me do it. You think it was, don't you?'

'I don't know.'

'I didn't believe you – but now this happened. What are you gonna do with it?'

'With what?'

'The head, you idiot.'

'I've thrown it away,' Rebecca whispered. 'I left it in the plastic bag and put it in the bin in the kitchen. I pushed it right down so Caroline wouldn't see it.'

'Nothing else can happen then?' said Jack.

'No, but I still want to find Caroline another figurine. Then she might trust us – and she might tell us about her and Mum. I want to know what happened.'

She looked up to see that Caroline was coming towards them across the ward, with a smiling nurse beside her.

'You'll have to take it easy for the next few days,' the nurse told Jack. 'No going out or running around – and no mischief-making either.'

She winked at Jack. Rebecca wondered what he'd been up to make her think he was a mischief-maker. She decided she'd rather not know.

Jack stood up, wincing as he put his weight on the bruised leg.

'That swelling and bruising should go down in a few days,' said the nurse, 'as long as you *rest*.'

Rebecca and Caroline helped him hobble out to the car.

'I'm going to look after you today,' Caroline told him, once they had set off. 'We'll give your sister a break and let her have some time to herself.'

Jack turned frantically to Rebecca who was sitting in the back. 'Becca doesn't mind staying with me, do you, Becca? You don't wanna go anywhere.'

'I . . .' Rebecca began, but Caroline interrupted.

'It's all settled, Jack – no argument.'

Jack gave Rebecca a desperate look. She shrugged.

They pulled up outside the house and Caroline went to open the front door.

'You won't really go out, will you?' Jack asked.

Rebecca hesitated. 'Just for a bit, Jack. I won't be long.'

Jack scowled.

'See you later then,' said Caroline. 'Will you be back for lunch?

'If that's okay?'

'Yes, yes – that'll be fine.'

''Bye, Jack,' Rebecca called.

'Becca!' Jack yelled. 'Becca! Come back here!'

Rebecca walked guiltily away from the house, down the sun-drenched path towards the beach. When she reached the promenade she stood breathing deeply for a while, staring at the calm sea, wishing she felt calmer herself.

She climbed down the steps and sat on the beach, running her hands through the pebbles beside her. She was away from Caroline, away from Jack, away from the china head. She had some space at last.

'I should feel happy,' she told herself – but now all she felt was an intense loneliness. She dug her hands into the pebbles. The ones on the surface were warm and dry, but a little way down they were cool and wet. She picked out a tiny one with a translucent, pinkish glow, and a smooth white one that looked like crystal. She became absorbed in picking out more pebbles – discarding rough, misshapen ones in favour of smooth, round pebbles that felt nice to touch.

'Hiya.'

Rebecca jumped at the voice so close to her ear. She looked round. It was Charlie.

'Where's Jack?' he asked.

Rebecca felt instantly hostile. *Jack.* Jack was all he cared about. But she knew this was unfair. It was an obvious question to ask.

'He had an accident, yesterday,' said Rebecca. 'He spent the night in hospital. He's with Caroline now.'

Charlie's eyes widened. 'Jeez, what happened?'

Rebecca explained.

'I wish I'd still been with you,' said Charlie. 'Maybe I could've stopped him . . . '

Rebecca glared at him. Why should he think he could have done any better than her?

'Or helped you, anyway.' Charlie's voice tailed off. He hovered awkwardly. 'Can I sit down?'

'It's a free country.'

Charlie shuffled down beside her. He saw the pebbles in her hand. 'They're nice. You can find amber on this beach sometimes.'

'Really?' Rebecca examined the pebbles more closely. She knew amber was an orangy colour but she wasn't sure exactly what it looked like.

'It's quite rare, I think,' Charlie warned her.

They sat silently for a few moments, Rebecca scanning the pebbles around her for anything that might be amber; Charlie staring out to sea.

'Do you want to walk a bit?' Charlie looked restless.

'Okay.' Rebecca didn't know what she wanted. She'd thought she wanted some time alone – but now she didn't want Charlie to go.

As they walked along, closer to the water's edge, a small orange pebble caught her eye.

She picked it up and the light shone through it. 'D'you think this one's amber?' she asked Charlie.

Charlie took it from her and examined it carefully. 'It might be. There's a way you can tell.' He reached into his pocket and pulled out an old bus ticket.

Rebecca watched curiously as he tore in into tiny pieces.

'Cup your hand,' he told her.

He tipped the torn paper into her cupped hand.

'What are you doing?' Rebecca asked, frowning.

Charlie rubbed the pebble against his T-shirt and then held it over her hand. 'If it's amber, the paper will jump up and cling to it,' he explained.

Rebecca held her breath.

The paper didn't cling.

'Better luck next time,' said Charlie.

'Yeh, right,' Rebecca said bitterly.

'We can look some more,' Charlie suggested. 'You never know.' He crouched down and began sifting through the pebbles by his feet.

Rebecca didn't join him, so he stopped and stood up again.

'Is Jack in bed, then?' he asked.

Rebecca wished he'd stop going on about Jack.

'He's not in bed exactly – but he is supposed to be resting,' she told Charlie. 'Caroline told me to go out and that she'd look after him. Jack went ballistic. I should probably go back now.'

'You shouldn't feel guilty about having a bit of time without him,' said Charlie.

Rebecca looked at him suspiciously. He was saying what she wanted to hear yet she felt instantly defensive. She'd been sure he would side with Jack.

She gave him a distrustful glare. 'You can't tell me what to feel.'

Charlie looked hurt. 'It's just...I should think you

could do with a break from him – especially after yesterday – anyone would. I don't know how you manage. I suppose it's easier at home with your mum. Did you say she was in hospital?'

'Not to you,' Rebecca thought. How did he know? He must have overheard them talking to Ray in the antique shop.

'Nothing serious, is it?' Charlie asked.

'Not what you think.'

Charlie looked puzzled. 'How do you know what I think?'

Rebecca felt a surge of anger at all his questions. 'Look – she's got a drug problem – heroin. She's in a clinic now, trying to get off it. Satisfied now?'

She put her hand over her mouth but she was too late – the words had already slipped out. How could she? How could she have told Charlie of all people? She could see his wide eyes and shocked expression.

'Jeez,' was all Charlie could muster.

Chapter 18

Rebecca jumped up, her heart pounding. 'I'd better go back now – see how Jack is.' She began to walk quickly back the way they'd come.

'No – wait,' Charlie pleaded. 'I shouldn't have asked you – I had no idea...'

'You won't want to be hanging around with me now,' said Rebecca, walking faster.

'Why not? It doesn't make any difference. Please – stay. You can tell me about it if you want to. Or if you don't want to talk about it that's fine. I won't ask any more questions, I promise. Please – don't go off.'

Rebecca stopped still. 'I can't believe I told you. I never told anyone – not even Nikita and she's my best friend.'

'Let's go down to that café by the pier and I'll buy you a drink,' said Charlie.

He began to walk and Rebecca followed numbly. He bought them both a Coke and they sat at a wooden picnic table outside. Rebecca said nothing. She didn't know what to say.

'I thought it was people our age who got into all that stuff,' said Charlie. 'I never heard of anyone's mum or dad doing it.'

'So did I until Mum,' said Rebecca. 'The whole thing's been a nightmare.'

'Do you...do you want to tell me about it?'

Rebecca met his eyes for the first time since her revelation. He looked kind and interested – not laughing at her like she feared.

'You won't tell your dad or anyone, will you? I couldn't bear it.'

'I won't tell a soul.'

Rebecca sipped her drink. 'I suppose it started when Jack's dad, Gary, left Mum. That was two and a half years ago. Mum got really stressed – we all did. Gary hadn't been paying the mortgage and we had to move out. We had nowhere to go and the council put us in this room in a homeless hostel. It was a complete nightmare. In the end they found us a flat on an estate. It wasn't as bad as the hostel but it was still dire.

'Mum was depressed for ages. It was like she couldn't be bothered with anything. Then about a year after we moved she met Mitch – and everything changed. He made her happy again and she was more like her old self. It was a big relief, I can tell you.

'I wasn't all that keen on Mitch. He could be moody sometimes. You never knew quite where you were with him. But at least he was making Mum happy. That was the main thing.

'We went on like that for a time – it must've been six months or more. Then I noticed Mum was sleeping a lot – and it worried me. She was kind of spaced out and she'd fall asleep sometimes, even when I was talking to her. It never went through my head for a minute that it was drugs, but she didn't seem right. I thought maybe she was getting depressed again.

'When I asked her if she was okay, she'd tell me not

to fuss and that she was fine. And then sometimes she did seem fine – really happy and laid back and I thought everything was getting back to normal.'

'So what happened?' Charlie asked.

'She started getting worse. Sometimes she couldn't get up in the mornings or anything. I had to get Jack up and ready for school – which wasn't easy, I'm telling you. She didn't seem to care what was going on. And Mitch wasn't much help. He'd moved in by then but he did shifts as a lorry driver so he wasn't there that much. He didn't seem to notice how Mum was. He used to get mad with Jack though – and Jack was playing up worse and worse. Then Mum lost her job in the shop – I don't know how she'd kept it so long seeing how she was.'

'How did you manage?' Charlie asked.

'We didn't manage really. I thought we were, but we weren't. Mum would just lie around the house all day and she'd even forget to do the shopping. We'd come home and the place would be a mess and Mum would be in bed or lying on the sofa or she'd be out and we wouldn't know where. And there'd be no food. Sometimes I ended up having to shop and cook and keep the place clean and do the washing and everything. And on top of that Jack was going off the rails and getting into trouble at school. I was struggling to get my homework done and I was getting some grief at school too.

'Then there was less and less money. I'd say I'd go and do the shopping after school but Mum would say she was out of cash. I thought it was just because she'd lost her job. Sometimes she'd bite my head off if I asked for money – even if it was for something I needed.'

Rebecca paused, screwing up her eyes in pain as she remembered. 'It was hell.'

'I can't even imagine,' said Charlie. 'It must've been awful. So how did you find out it was drugs?'

'I must've been thick not to work it out, but it never went through my head. I had no idea. Then one day – last February, it was raining really hard and I was trying to keep Jack occupied. I was looking for a game I knew we had and I couldn't find it. I got a stool and looked on the top of Mum's wardrobe, thinking it might be there. This bag fell down and a couple of syringes fell out.'

'That might not have meant drugs, though,' said Charlie. 'She could've been diabetic or something.'

'She'd have told me that, wouldn't she?' said Rebecca. 'And anyway – it reminded me of something – a while ago – there were some kids at school who were going round saying my dad was a dealer. Back then I was more fussed that they thought Mitch was my dad. I thought the stuff about dealing was rubbish they'd made up – because that's what they're like – make up a story about you and start spreading rumours so everyone believes it. I'd seen them do it before.'

Charlie nodded. 'There's people like that at my school too.'

'And we'd had some lessons on drugs at school,' Rebecca continued. 'When I thought about it, how Mum was – it all made sense. And I was sure Mitch was dealing. I reckoned he must be supplying Mum with stuff.'

'So what did you do?' Charlie asked. 'I don't know what I'd have done.'

'I didn't do anything at first. I didn't know what to do. I wanted to talk to someone but I thought Mum might get in trouble and that we might end up in care. I was so scared. In the end – I just asked Mum straight out. I told her I knew.'

'What happened?' Charlie asked, leaning forward.

'It was awful. She denied it – acted like she was horrified that I could even think it. She said the syringes must've been there before we moved in and they were nothing to do with her. She said she'd been a bit tired lately – that was all.

'I didn't know what to do then. I thought maybe what she said was true. I didn't want to believe my mum would lie to me like that.

'Then, in March, Mitch got arrested. He was dealing from a flat the other side of the estate – and he had a load of gear on him. The police came round and searched our place but they never found anything. Mum was really shaken up about it. After they'd gone she sat on the sofa and cried and cried. I asked her again about the drugs, and in the end she admitted it. She hugged me and she said said she'd only been using heroin to help her feel calmer and she could stop anytime. She promised she'd never take drugs again in her life and she'd get another job – and everything would be okay.

'A few days later social services sent someone round. I don't know if the police had said anything but I know Jack's school had put them onto us because he was still getting into trouble and Mum hadn't turned up to the meetings they'd arranged with his teacher. The social worker, Denise, seemed nice but I was really scared they might put us in care. Denise said she would have to keep a close eye on us and she persuaded Mum to go to the doctor.

'I don't know what the doctor said, but Mum came back very cheerful and said I shouldn't worry – she was making a fresh start and everything would be fine from now on.'

'But it wasn't that easy?' Charlie asked. 'It can't have been if she's in a clinic now.'

Rebecca nodded. 'She'd go a few hours – that's all. Then she'd start feeling sick and she'd get all shaky. I'd come home from school and find her like that. She looked so ill I was really frightened. But she said she'd get through it. She promised. Then later she'd be all relaxed and sleepy and I knew she'd had another fix. She couldn't make it through one whole day without heroin. Every day she just promised she'd try again tomorrow. She was a right mess.

'Every time Denise was coming round I was terrified Jack would play up or Mum would be in a state and I thought we'd end up in care – but Mum managed to put on a good act and so did Jack and somehow we got through it.

'Then a few weeks ago, just before school broke up, I came home and found Mum completely out of it on the sofa. I couldn't wake her up. I was so scared, I can't tell you. I reckon she'd overdosed or had a bad cut – dealers mix up heroin with all kinds of stuff so it looks more. You never know what's in it. I thought she was going to die. I called an ambulance – but Mum came round before the ambulance arrived. She said no way was she going to hospital. She was angry that I'd called them. Sometimes I still feel guilty...'

Rebecca paused.

'What else could you have done?' said Charlie. 'I don't see that you had any choice. You weren't going to sit by and let her die, were you?'

Rebecca felt comforted by his words. She knew really – but it was reassuring to hear it from someone else.

'I know,' she continued. 'It was the only thing I could do. But when they came, the ambulance people couldn't make Mum go with them. She kicked up a right fuss. So instead, the doctor came round, and Denise.

'They went and talked to Mum for ages in the other room, and then Denise came and told me and Jack that Mum had to go in a clinic to help her get off the drugs. She said Mum had been on a waiting list since she saw the doctor and they'd managed to find her a place. It was the first I'd heard of it. And she said we had to go into care for a few weeks – just till Mum got better. I couldn't believe it. I said no way was I going into care. I thought if we went into care they'd never let us back with Mum.

'I was crying and then Mum started crying. That was when she suddenly said she had a sister. That's Caroline – we never knew she existed before. Mum hadn't talked to her for years. I still don't know why. Mum rang her and she said she'd have us – so that's how we ended up here.'

'It must have been terrible.'

Rebecca felt the tears begin to stream down her face. 'I can't believe I told you all that.'

'I'm glad you told me.'

'And I don't know if the clinic will help. Mum sounded weird when she phoned.'

'I guess she's bound to feel worse first, isn't she, before she feels better? At least she's getting some help now – and that's down to you calling that ambulance.'

'I suppose.' Rebecca paused. 'And Caroline never wanted us here. If it wasn't for me making such a fuss about being in care we might be with a nice foster family now who wanted us – and who could handle Jack.'

'And who didn't have collections of antique china?' Charlie added.

'Yes – right.' She tried to smile but her mouth wasn't in the mood.

'You are still coming with me to that antiques fair tomorrow?' Charlie asked.

'I suppose. We'll never find a figurine like Caroline's, though, will we?'

'We might – you never know. I'll meet you at the bus stop opposite the shop at half past nine. Will that be okay?'

'If you like.' Rebecca sniffed and wiped her eyes. 'Look – I'd better get back and see how Jack's doing. I oughtn't to leave him too long – he'll kill me. Do you think there's a loo round here?'

'Round the back, past the arcade,' said Charlie.

Rebecca went into the toilets and splashed water on her face. She didn't want Jack or Caroline to see she'd been crying.

'Do I look okay?' she asked Charlie, when she got back to where he was standing waiting.

'You look lovely,' he said.

Rebecca felt herself blush. 'No – I mean could you tell I've been crying?'

'You'd never know. Listen – do you want me to come with you? I'd like to see Jack.'

'If you come back with me, he might forgive me for going off,' said Rebecca. 'But I don't know about Caroline . . . '

'Let's give it a go – if she doesn't look keen I won't hang around.'

'I bet she's wishing she never said she'd look after him,' said Rebecca, as they approached the house.

Chapter 19

To Rebecca's surprise, Caroline opened the door looking more cheerful than she could remember.

'Charlie's come to see Jack,' Rebecca explained. 'Is that okay?'

'Yes, yes – come in,' said Caroline.

'We've been getting along nicely,' she told Rebecca, as she led the way towards the kitchen. 'Jack's very interested in history, isn't he?'

'Is he?' Rebecca said doubtfully.

'I've been telling him about the time the whole town burned down. 1659, that was. When they rebuilt, they designed the town with seven greens so that a fire could never spread like that again.'

'I never knew that,' said Charlie.

'Then we went on to castles,' Caroline continued. 'I found a book about them with some pictures in it. Most of my books don't have pictures, you see. I found some card – Jack's making a castle, aren't you, Jack?'

Jack was sitting at the kitchen table, surrounded by cardboard, sellotape and scissors.

'Charlie!' he exclaimed, ignoring Rebecca completely. 'Do you want to see my leg? I've got a whopping bruise.'

'Maybe later,' said Charlie. 'What's this you're making?'

if she was trying to look deeper into it. Rebecca tried to follow her gaze. It wasn't the people Caroline seemed to be looking at – it was the background – the beach hut behind them.

'That beach hut,' Rebecca said with sudden interest. 'Was it yours?' It hadn't occurred to Rebecca when they'd looked at the photos before. But the family was sitting in front of the open beach hut, looking as if they owned it.

'It was.' Caroline's voice sounded stiff.

'Is it still?' Jack asked with excitement. 'Is it still yours? Can we use it?'

'No, it's not mine,' Caroline snapped, 'not anymore. It had to be sold.'

'Why?' Jack demanded.

'Enough!' Caroline shrieked. 'I can't take any more of this!' She grabbed the album from Jack, slammed it shut and stormed out of the room and up the stairs.

Rebecca laid her head on the kitchen table.

'That went well, didn't it?' she said sarcastically.

'She didn't like you asking her about that beach hut,' said Jack.

'I only asked because she was looking at it in the photo – I'm sure she was.'

Jack kicked at the table leg. 'I wish she did still have it and we could use it. That'd be great.'

'I don't know why she had to get so upset about it,' said Rebccca. 'We can't ask her anything without her throwing a wobbly.'

'I'd be upset if I had one of those beach huts and I had to sell it,' said Jack.

'It wasn't just that though, was it? It's about her and Mum and everything. I'm sure it is.'

Jack frowned. 'You think Mum made her sell it?'

'I don't know, do I?'

Caroline didn't reappear. Jack looked tired and hobbled up to bed without the usual protest. Rebecca wasn't far behind him. She read for a while before turning out the light.

She slept quickly but woke with an instant sinking feeling. She knew straight away – she felt awake, but she wasn't. She was back in the horrific dream world that had terrified her once before. And the giant china figures were back too. As they gathered round the bed she was desperate to escape. But their bitter faces loomed in towards her, full of rage.

'Wake up, wake up!' she urged herself. She wanted to pull back – pull away, or at least pull the duvet up over her head. But again – like the last time, she couldn't move. The faces came closer and closer. She could feel their fury. And this time she knew it was *her* they were angry with – not Jack. It was because she had thrown away the head. That must be it. She had insulted them. They would not rest until they had their friend back in one piece.

'It was too badly broken,' she tried to explain to them. No sound came out of her mouth, yet she sensed they could hear her thoughts. 'There's no way of fixing it. I'm doing everything I can to replace it – that's all I can do. And I don't need the head to do that. I know what the figure looked like. I'm trying my best. I know you're upset about it. I'm upset too. Please go, please – leave me alone.'

'I'm copying the castle in this book. He unburied the book and held it up. 'D'you want to help?'

'I think we'd better clear it away while we have some lunch, Jack,' said Caroline. 'You can carry on later.'

She turned to Charlie. 'You will stay for lunch, won't you?'

'If you're sure?'

Rebecca and Charlie cleared the table between them, carrying Jack's creation and materials over to a space on the floor.

'Be careful,' Jack instructed from his seat. 'I'll murder you if you break it.'

Caroline had made a big tuna salad for lunch. To Rebecca's surprise Jack ate most of it without protest (apart from the tomato, of course).

After lunch Rebecca and Charlie helped Jack with his castle for a while. Then she walked Charlie back to his place, leaving Jack still working on his castle. When she got back, Caroline said Jack was having a nap in the lounge, while she got on with some work in her study.

Rebecca peeped round the lounge door, not wanting to disturb Jack if he was asleep, but rather doubtful that he would be. There was no sign of Jack in the lounge. She tried the kitchen, and the toilet. Anxiously, she even tried the door to the room of china figures, but was relieved to find it locked. Where was he? Perhaps he'd decided he'd rather rest in his room, even if it did mean climbing the stairs with his painful leg.

Jack wasn't in his room. She listened, but could hear

no sounds apart from Caroline typing at the computer in her study.

'Jack,' she whispered.

A door suddenly opened. 'Becca – get in here quick!'

'What the hell are you doing?' Rebecca demanded, joining him in a small bedroom, empty apart from a bed with bare mattress, and a tall wardrobe. 'I thought you were supposed to be having a lie-down?'

'I didn't feel like it. I was having a look round and I came in here. I saw this wardrobe and I thought it would be a laugh to hide in there.' He gave a mischievous smirk.

'*Hide*?' Rebecca repeated. 'We'd never have found you.'

'It was only for a laugh. I'm bored, that's all.'

'I thought you and Caroline were turning into best mates,' said Rebecca. 'And what happened to that castle you were making?'

'I'll do it later. Caroline said I should have a rest. I think she'd had enough of me. Anyway – you're not listening. I was trying to tell you about the wardrobe.'

'What about it? It looks pretty ordinary to me.'

'It's not the wardrobe – it's what's inside.'

'What?'

Jack pulled one of the double doors open, and stood back.

The wardrobe was chock-full of dresses, some black and some more brightly coloured, all hanging in polythene wrappers.

'Dresses. So what?' said Rebecca.

'And look at this one.' Jack pulled open the other wardrobe door. At the far end hung a very bulky, lacy white dress. Even through the polythene, it was unmistakably a wedding dress.

Rebecca looked at it more closely. It had a tight bodice and full skirt, the sleeves, neck and frill of the dress were all lace. 'It's beautiful.'

'Do you think it's hers?' Jack asked.

'Caroline's? How can it be – she's not married.'

'Then why's she got it in here?'

'I don't know, do I? Maybe it was her mum's. She lived here too, didn't she?'

Rebecca looked again at the dress. It didn't look all that old.

'Maybe she was married and she got divorced,' Jack suggested.

'I wouldn't want to keep my wedding dress if I'd got divorced,' said Rebecca. 'Come on – Caroline might go and check on you in the lounge any minute. You'd better get back down there.'

Jack watched as Rebecca closed the wardrobe doors. 'It's weird, isn't it?'

'I suppose.' Everything was weird. Rebecca felt she was collecting weird things just like Caroline collected china figures and Charlie antique cars.

'I'll ask Caroline about the photos in that album,' Jack suggested. 'Maybe that'll start her talking. And she is in a good mood, isn't she?'

'Yes – but she won't be for much longer if she finds us in here – or sees you're not resting in the lounge. Come on.'

Chapter 20

They waited until evening to ask Caroline about the photos. Rebecca let Jack do the talking.

'We found this in that box of books you gave us,' he told her.

Caroline stiffened visibly and stared at the album.

'Thank you,' she said, holding out her hand to take it. 'I don't know how that ended up in there. I'll put it away.'

Jack pulled the album back towards his chest. 'Will you tell us about the people – the ones in the photos?'

Without waiting for a reply he opened the album and found a picture of the baby.

'Is that our mum?' he asked holding it so Caroline could see. 'Only, we've never seen any pictures of Mum when she was little . . . '

Caroline frowned.

'Please,' Rebecca begged. 'We've never seen any photos of our grandparents either. We only want to know about them. There's nothing wrong with that, is there?'

'I suppose not.' Caroline moved her face nearer to the picture.

Rebecca thought she looked a little afraid.

'Yes, that's your mum all right.' She turned the page. 'And these are our parents – your grandparents. Dad was already ill then – you can see it in his face.'

Caroline went quiet. She was staring at the photo, as

if she was trying to look deeper into it. Rebecca tried to follow her gaze. It wasn't the people Caroline seemed to be looking at – it was the background – the beach hut behind them.

'That beach hut,' Rebecca said with sudden interest. 'Was it yours?' It hadn't occurred to Rebecca when they'd looked at the photos before. But the family was sitting in front of the open beach hut, looking as if they owned it.

'It was.' Caroline's voice sounded stiff.

'Is it still?' Jack asked with excitement. 'Is it still yours? Can we use it?'

'No, it's not mine,' Caroline snapped, 'not anymore. It had to be sold.'

'Why?' Jack demanded.

'Enough!' Caroline shrieked. 'I can't take any more of this!' She grabbed the album from Jack, slammed it shut and stormed out of the room and up the stairs.

Rebecca laid her head on the kitchen table.

'That went well, didn't it?' she said sarcastically.

'She didn't like you asking her about that beach hut,' said Jack.

'I only asked because she was looking at it in the photo – I'm sure she was.'

Jack kicked at the table leg. 'I wish she did still have it and we could use it. That'd be great.'

'I don't know why she had to get so upset about it,' said Rebecca. 'We can't ask her anything without her throwing a wobbly.'

'I'd be upset if I had one of those beach huts and I had to sell it,' said Jack.

'It wasn't just that though, was it? It's about her and Mum and everything. I'm sure it is.'

Jack frowned. 'You think Mum made her sell it?'

'I don't know, do I?'

Caroline didn't reappear. Jack looked tired and hobbled up to bed without the usual protest. Rebecca wasn't far behind him. She read for a while before turning out the light.

She slept quickly but woke with an instant sinking feeling. She knew straight away – she felt awake, but she wasn't. She was back in the horrific dream world that had terrified her once before. And the giant china figures were back too. As they gathered round the bed she was desperate to escape. But their bitter faces loomed in towards her, full of rage.

'Wake up, wake up!' she urged herself. She wanted to pull back – pull away, or at least pull the duvet up over her head. But again – like the last time, she couldn't move. The faces came closer and closer. She could feel their fury. And this time she knew it was *her* they were angry with – not Jack. It was because she had thrown away the head. That must be it. She had insulted them. They would not rest until they had their friend back in one piece.

'It was too badly broken,' she tried to explain to them. No sound came out of her mouth, yet she sensed they could hear her thoughts. 'There's no way of fixing it. I'm doing everything I can to replace it – that's all I can do. And I don't need the head to do that. I know what the figure looked like. I'm trying my best. I know you're upset about it. I'm upset too. Please go, please – leave me alone.'

The figures leaned in further, a mass of heads, their vengeful faces pressed up close to hers. She could feel their ice-cold touch and there was no space for her to breathe.

She woke in a shivery sweat – gasping for breath. She sat up quickly and switched on the bedside light. It was 3am. There were no china figures – round the bed or anywhere. They were locked up – in the room downstairs. It was just a dream.

'I must be having these dreams because I feel guilty that Caroline's figurine got broken, that's all,' she told herself. 'I'm going to the antiques fair with Charlie to try and find her one. I'm doing everything I can.'

She turned out the light and tried to sleep again. It was no good. She tried reading for a while but couldn't concentrate. The image of the china head had fixed itself on her brain. She couldn't get it out of her mind.

'I have to get it back,' she finally decided. 'I'll go down and get the head out of the bin. I'll keep it in the plastic bag, I won't touch it or anything. That'll stop them being so angry.'

She tried once more to remind herself that it was only a dream – the china figures couldn't really be upset. China figures didn't have feelings. But she knew she had to get it back. She stood up and slid her feet into slippers.

Downstairs she turned on the kitchen light and pushed the pedal bin open with her toe. An empty white bin liner met her eyes. Caroline had put out the rubbish. Rebecca swore. She unlocked the front door and made her way round the side to the wheelie bin. The night air was chilly and it was very dark. She shivered. There were two rubbish sacks in the bin. She tried to reach to pull open the top one. It was tightly tied and her fingers were too cold. She couldn't see what she was doing.

'It's hopeless,' she told herself. 'I'll never find it.'

She left the bin and hurried back inside and upstairs, washing her hands in the bathroom before climbing back into bed. She snuggled down, glad of the comfort of the duvet after the cold, dark night.

She wondered if she should have tried harder to search through the rubbish. But she drifted off to sleep, and when she woke at 6am she could hear the noise of a dustvan outside. It was too late now.

Chapter 21

In the morning, as Rebecca got dressed, her mind was still in a whirl from the dream. She had to get another figurine – that was all she could think about.

Jack came into the room. 'Becca, you're not going out, are you? You can't leave me with Caroline – not like she was last night.'

'I'm going to the antiques fair,' said Rebecca. 'You know I am.'

'You can't – not without me – it's not fair!' Jack protested. 'I'll come with – I'm not staying here with her.'

'Everything doesn't just revolve around you, Jack,' said Rebecca. 'I'll bring Charlie back here after – all right? You know you can't go out with your leg like that. I'm sure Caroline will be okay. You can finish off that castle.'

'You'll bring Charlie?' said Jack. 'You promise?'

'Yes, I promise.'

Caroline didn't look too keen on Rebecca going out, but she didn't argue, to Rebecca's relief.

'I have to find a china figure like Caroline's,' Rebecca told Charlie, as they waited for the bus to Halesworth. 'You don't know how important it is – I have to find one, I have to.'

Charlie looked puzzled. 'Is your aunt still mad about it? I thought she'd got over it – she seemed happy enough when I was there yesterday.'

'We have to get one – I'm telling you,' Rebecca insisted. 'Something bad will happen otherwise. You must believe me.'

'All right – I get the picture,' said Charlie, who clearly didn't get it at all. 'We'll do our best.'

Rebecca was feeling desperate now. She knew she was being driven by the frightening dreams of the night, and the strange things that had happened around the china head. She was trying not to let those things get to her – to tell herself they weren't real. But they felt too real now – it was beyond a joke.

'We will find one, won't we?' she asked.

'I can't promise anything,' said Charlie, 'but if we don't find one today – there's always tomorrow or the next day. I'll help you as much as I can.'

'And if we do find one, how will we pay for it?' Rebecca asked. 'I thought your dad would be coming. He did mean it about paying if we find one, didn't he?'

'Stop stressing out, will you?' said Charlie. He sounded irritated. 'I've got my mobile. If we find anything I'll ring Dad. It'll be fine.'

Rebecca shut up after that.

When they reached the community centre in Halesworth, and entered the hall where the antiques fair was on, her hopes went up dramatically. It was far bigger than she'd imagined. The large room was crammed with trestle tables; an outer ring and an inner ring. Each table was an Aladdin's cave of antiques – jewellery, books, crockery, silver, toys and all kinds of other things.

Rebecca was eager to rush round the whole fair in the hope that any china figures might catch her eye. Charlie was more for the systematic approach – examining the contents of each stand carefully before moving on to the next. Rebecca followed him impatiently.

'There's nothing here – let's try that one over there,' she suggested, pointing to a distant stall.

'If we don't go round them in order we won't know which ones we've seen and which ones we haven't,' Charlie pointed out. 'Stick with me and then we'll be sure not to miss anything.'

When there weren't many more tables to see, Rebecca's hope began to fade. They'd found a few small china dolls and figures, but they hadn't come across anything remotely like Caroline's.

She felt defeated. 'We're not going to find one, are we?'

'I didn't promise anything,' said Charlie.

'But...'

Charlie didn't let her speak. He pointed to a life-size ceramic dog, that was incredibly ugly. 'Do you think your aunt would like one of those?' he teased.

'Imagine her face if I came back with that!' Rebecca couldn't help laughing.

They carried on round, searching each stand carefully. It was only when they reached the last but one table, that something caught Rebecca's eye. 'Did you see that, Charlie?'

'Where?'

Rebecca pointed to a little red car, which was sitting on top of its box.

'It's got the box, too,' she said, still finding it hard to

believe that the box should be so important.

Charlie picked up the car and examined it casually. He didn't look very impressed.

'Is it any good?' she asked. 'I wouldn't know. I just saw it and thought...'

The price label said fifteen pounds. Charlie put the car back.

The woman behind the table stood up and leant forward. 'I could do you that for thirteen fifty?' she offered.

Charlie picked up the car again.

'Nah, I don't think so,' he said, shrugging.

'Twelve?' the woman suggested.

'Ten?' Charlie bargained – sounding vaguely interested in the car for the first time.

The woman was quiet for a moment. 'Eleven, and that's my final price,' she announced.

'I'll take it,' said Charlie, pulling out his wallet.

Rebecca looked at him in surprise. 'Why are you buying it if you don't really like it?' she asked.

Charlie said nothing until they had checked out the final table and were out of the hall.

'I do like it,' he said, grinning broadly. 'And it's a great price for one of these in mint condition. I've not seen one for less than £25. I didn't want the woman to see how keen I was or she'd never have dropped the price.'

'So you really like it?' Rebecca asked.

'Yes! I love it!' He squeezed her hand. 'Thank you for spotting it – I was so set on looking for a figurine for you I wasn't even thinking about cars. Look – I'm sorry we didn't find one.'

'So am I,' said Rebecca. Panic ran through her as the

dream came back into her mind. What was she going to do? She wished she could talk to Charlie about it but she knew it would all sound too crazy.

'Dad's doing a house clearance tomorrow,' said Charlie. 'Maybe you can come along. I'd have thought this antiques fair would have been a better bet, but you never know.'

'What's a house clearance?' Rebecca asked.

'Some old biddy's died and Dad's got to clear her house. The relatives take anything they want and then Dad gives them a price for the rest of the stuff. He chucks the rubbish, sells on the bric-à-brac and keeps anything worth selling for the shop.'

'Isn't it creepy – going in a house where someone's died?'

'Nah.' Charlie screwed up his face. 'Never think about it really.'

'I'll come if there's a chance of finding a figurine like Caroline's,' she said. 'I have to do anything I can.'

'I'd better check with Dad first,' said Charlie. 'But I'm sure he won't mind.'

They took the bus back to Southwold.

'Do you fancy a walk along the river?' Charlie asked.

Rebecca hesitated. She was in no hurry to get back to Jack and Caroline. 'I suppose it'll be all right – if we're not too long.'

The river was peaceful and calming, and Rebecca was glad she'd agreed to the walk. Their conversation dropped off but it didn't seem to matter. Rebecca felt comfortable with Charlie. Along the riverbank people were fishing. One man turned and looked up as they passed.

'Bill!' Rebecca exclaimed.

'Caroline's niece, isn't it?' said Bill. 'Sorry I don't know your name.'

'Rebecca,' she told him. 'And this is Charlie, a friend of mine.'

Bill nodded to Charlie and then turned back to Rebecca. 'She forgiven you for that ornament of hers?'

'I don't think so – not completely,' said Rebecca.

'Well, give her my best regards, anyway,' said Bill, as if eager to end the conversation. 'Washing machine's okay now, I hope?'

'Yes – I think so,' said Rebecca.

Bill turned back towards the river.

Rebecca hesitated. His mentioning the washing machine had brought something back into her mind. When they'd come back to find the kitchen flooded, Caroline had been talking to Bill about what Mum had done. Maybe he knew. This was her chance to ask him. She might not see him again.

'Bill,' she began. He turned back to face her.

'You know what happened between Caroline and my mum, don't you?'

Bill hesitated. 'I know all right,' he admitted, looking at her warily.

'Please tell me,' Rebecca begged.

Bill coughed. 'Look, love. I always think honesty's the best policy but if your mum and aunt don't want you to know, it's not my place to start telling you, is it?'

'Will you just answer yes or no to one question, then?' Rebecca tried.

'That depends,' Bill said cautiously.

'Was Caroline ever married?' Rebecca asked.

Bill looked surprised at the question. 'No,' he said. 'Oh – I've got a bite!'

He turned back to the river, frantically reeling in his line. They watched as he pulled up a flailing fish.

'That'll do nicely for my tea,' he said, smiling.

Charlie turned to Rebecca. 'We'd better get back, hadn't we?'

They began to walk towards the town.

'Did you see his face when I asked if Caroline was ever married?' said Rebecca.

'Yes – I reckon he must have been in love with her once – don't you think?'

Rebecca was startled. 'In love with Caroline? He's a bit old, isn't he?'

'It's possible though.'

Rebecca laughed and Charlie grinned. 'You never know.'

'Are you coming back with me, to see Jack?' she asked.

'I would – but Dad needs a hand with something this afternoon. Do you mind if I give it a miss? Come round to my place in the morning and we'll see what Dad says about the house clearance.'

'Thanks, Charlie,' said Rebecca. 'I'll see you tomorrow, then.'

Chapter 22

When she got back to Caroline's, Rebecca sensed the atmosphere and immediately felt guilty.

'I'm sorry I was so long – I lost track of time,' she told Caroline. 'Is everything okay?'

'Yes,' Caroline said frostily. 'Jack's been a bit restless, that's all. I assume you've had lunch out.'

Rebecca didn't like to say she hadn't, so she nodded.

'Where've you been, Becca?' said Jack. 'You were gone ages.'

'You finished your castle, then?' Rebecca asked, deliberately changing the subject.

Jack's castle looked rather the worse for wear. The card was too thin and the walls and turrets were all leaning at strange angles.

'I finished it hours ago and there was nothing else to do,' Jack said bitterly. 'And where's Charlie? Why didn't you bring him here? You promised.'

'He's doing something with his dad,' said Rebecca. 'Maybe he'll come and see you tomorrow.'

Caroline was looking worried. 'I hope you're not getting up to any hanky-panky with that boy.'

Rebecca felt her face redden. 'Of course not,' she said angrily. 'He's just a friend, that's all.'

'He's my friend, not yours,' Jack retorted. 'You said you didn't even like him.'

'Shut up, Jack,' said Rebecca.

'Enough – both of you!' Caroline exclaimed. 'Now I have some work to get on with.' She looked at Rebecca. 'You'll be okay with Jack for the rest of the afternoon, won't you?'

Rebecca nodded. Once they were alone, she told Jack about the antiques fair.

'It's a waste of time looking if you ask me,' said Jack. 'I never thought you'd find one anyway.'

Rebecca was silent. She wanted to tell him about the nightmares but she couldn't.

'I bumped into Bill,' she said. 'I tried to ask him things but he wasn't giving much away. He did say Caroline was never married, though.'

'So why's she got that wedding dress?' Jack asked.

'Charlie reckons Caroline might've had a thing going with Bill once,' Rebecca told him. 'He certainly looked iffy when he said she was never married.'

'*Caroline and Bill*?' said Jack, screwing up his face in disgust.

'It's a crazy idea, isn't it?' Rebecca admitted. 'And it doesn't give us any clues about what happened between Caroline and Mum.'

'When you were out, Caroline started asking about Dad,' Jack told her.

'Your dad?' Rebecca asked.

'Yes – well, no,' said Jack. 'She never even knew we had different dads.'

Rebecca thought about this. 'We never knew she existed, did we? If Mum didn't talk to her all those years, she probably knows as much about us as we do about her.'

'You're right – she doesn't know a thing,' said Jack.

Rebecca felt curious. 'What was she asking?'

Jack rested his chin on his hand, trying to remember. 'She asked when Mum left Dad.'

'When Mum left Dad?' Rebecca repeated, screwing up her face. 'But it was Dad who left Mum – both our dads. Why was she asking that?'

'I don't know. She got a bit confused when I was trying to explain. Then she went all quiet. I think she thought Neil was my dad too. I said it doesn't make any difference to us. You're my sister.'

'If she and Mum stopped talking all those years ago,' Rebecca said thoughtfully, 'then she probably only knew about Neil. She wouldn't have known about Gary. She might not even have known we existed until Mum phoned her.'

'D'you reckon?' said Jack. 'I told her I don't know nothing about Neil. You don't know much either, do you? Don't you wonder about him? He is your dad.'

'Mum never wants to talk about him,' said Rebecca. 'She says he was a bad piece of work. He left her when she was pregnant, didn't he? He didn't want to know me, so why should I want to know about him?'

Rebecca lay in bed that night, afraid to go to sleep in case the nightmares returned. Exhausted but restless she finally got up to go to the toilet. She crept quietly up the dark stairs and into the bathroom, reaching for the light switch. Something rustled below her foot, startling her. She turned the light on and stared down.

On the bathroom floor was a scrunched blue plastic

bag. It looked exactly like the bag that had contained the china head. But it couldn't be the same bag – could it? She'd pushed that bag deep into the bin in the kitchen; Caroline had emptied the bin; the dustvan had taken the rubbish away.

What was a bag doing there anyway? It hadn't been there when she'd brushed her teeth. She pushed at it with her toe. There was something inside – a small round lump in one corner. 'Am I dreaming?' she wondered, rubbing her eyes.

She reached down cautiously and picked up the bag, pulling the sides apart to reveal the contents. When she saw the china head inside, she was gripped by terror. It couldn't be. It wasn't possible. Her hands began to shake, making the head jerk in the bag, so it looked as if writhing about in pain.

'No!' she cried out, unable to stop herself. 'No! No! No!'

She half-expected to wake up – to find herself in bed – to know it was just a nightmare. But she was still standing there. The blue bag with the china head was still in her hand.

Chapter 23

Rebecca's cries must have been loud because within seconds Caroline and Jack were outside the bathroom. Caroline's messy hair and wide eyes made her look witch-like, while her white cotton nightie gave her a ghostly glow in the bathroom light. Jack stood gaping in his too-short pyjamas, screwing up his face as his eyes adjusted to the brightness.

'What on earth's the matter?' Caroline demanded, her voice shrill and anxious. 'Are you ill?'

Rebecca couldn't speak. She shivered uncontrollably, and the now closed bag rustled, as if crying out to be noticed.

Caroline and Jack looked at the bag.

'Becca . . . ' Jack whispered.

'What have you got there?' Caroline asked.

Rebecca was still silent.

'What's going on?' Caroline said impatiently. 'Talk to me.'

'She'll be all right,' Jack told Caroline, sounding as if he was the adult and she the child. 'You go back to bed. I'll talk to her.'

Caroline didn't move. 'What's in the bag? Give it to me.'

She pulled the bag from Rebecca's hand and opened it. As the head revealed itself, she gasped. She stared down at it in disbelief. Then she looked up and glared at them both.

When she spoke her voice trembled, full of hurt and anger. 'I don't – I don't know what games you two have been up to, but this is too much. You are cruel, cruel children, both of you. Nothing but trouble you've brought me. As if your mother didn't cause me enough pain, she had to send you two to finish the job off. I can't bear it. I just can't bear it.'

Still clutching the bag, she turned and disappeared down the stairs, loud rasping sobs accompanying her footsteps.

Rebecca and Jack stood in the bathroom, Rebecca still shaking; Jack watching her.

'Are you okay?' Jack asked.

'It doesn't make sense,' Rebecca muttered, shaking her head slowly. 'How did it get here, Jack? I threw it away. It can't have come back on its own. I feel like I'm going mad.'

'Becca . . . ' Jack began hesitantly.

'What?'

'I never meant all this to happen.'

'What are you talking about?'

Jack leant back against the bathroom wall. 'It was me.'

Rebecca frowned. 'What do you mean, it was you?'

'You know you said you put it in the kitchen bin? Well, I took it out again.'

'You did what?'

'I took it out – that day we came back from the hospital. I wanted to keep it. I thought it might be useful, that's all.'

'For what?' Rebecca couldn't understand what he was saying.

Jack wriggled sheepishly. 'You know Daniel Hooper and Dean Rudd at my school? They're real bullies they are. I thought I could get them with that head – so they'd leave me alone. I could tell them it was cursed and dare them to hold it. They'd do it 'cos they wouldn't believe me. Then I'd just wait to see the damage. You know, to see it hurt them like it hurt me.'

'You were going to do that?' Rebecca looked at him in disbelief.

Jack nodded.

'What I don't understand,' Rebecca continued, 'is how it ended up on the bathroom floor in the middle of the night.'

'I had it under the bed in my room,' Jack explained, 'but it was giving me the jitters. I couldn't get to sleep and I didn't know what to do with it. I was only leaving it in here for the night. I was gonna move it in the morning before you saw it. I didn't mean you to find it like that.'

'And now Caroline . . . ' said Rebecca.

'It's not my fault you started yelling like that and she came up,' Jack said defensively.

'Nothing's ever your fault, is it?' Rebecca glared at him. 'She probably thinks we kept the head so we could torment her with it. D'you realise that, Jack?'

'We can still try and get her another one,' Jack suggested timidly.

'Yeh, right,' Rebecca snapped.

They went back to bed, though neither of them seemed likely to sleep after what had happened. Rebecca lay sobbing into the pillow, until it was so wet she had to turn it over.

The most unfair thing was that every time Jack did something stupid, Caroline decided to blame them both. Surely it had been obvious that Rebecca hadn't had anything to do with it. She felt full of anger – with Caroline, with Jack – and even with Mum for getting in such a state that they'd ended up here.

In the morning Caroline was as frosty with them as she'd been after the figurine was first broken. The only sound over breakfast was that of spoons clanking against bowls. Rebecca looked uneasily at Caroline.

'Is it okay if I go out for a bit this morning?' she asked nervously.

'Yes, fine,' Caroline said gruffly.

Rebecca heaved a sigh of relief. She was determined to go the house clearance with Charlie.

Jack gave her a furious look. 'But, Becca, you...'

Caroline interrupted. 'You'll have to take Jack with you. I'm not having him wreaking havoc in this house any longer.'

Rebecca's heart sank. There was no way Ray would let Jack come with them to the house clearance. She looked at Caroline pleadingly. 'But he's supposed to still be resting.'

'I don't need any more rest – I'm fine now,' Jack insisted.

'He hasn't been doing much resting as it is,' said Caroline. 'I think it'll be a good idea if you both get out from under my hair, especially after last night.'

Jack looked delighted. 'We can go and see Charlie! Come on, Becca.'

'All right,' said Rebecca. It didn't look as if she had much choice.

Chapter 24

Charlie grinned as he opened the door to Rebecca. 'Dad says you can come with us,' he said.

'Surprise!' cried Jack, leaping out from behind Rebecca.

Charlie's face fell a little.

'Where's your dad say we can go?' Jack asked. He clearly hadn't noticed Charlie's expression.

Rebecca met Charlie's eyes and held her hands up in a helpless gesture.

'Come and sit in the lounge,' said Charlie. 'I need to talk to Dad for a minute.'

'Sorry,' Rebecca whispered, as Charlie opened the lounge door. 'Caroline got upset with us last night and she chucked us both out of the house this morning.'

Charlie gave her a wink, as if to say he would try to sort it all out. Then he left them in the lounge.

Jack made himself at home and turned on the TV. Rebecca sat down on the edge of the sofa.

When Charlie came back in he was smiling. 'I persuaded Dad,' he told Rebecca. 'You can both come.'

'Come where?' Jack asked.

'Are you sure it's a good idea?' said Rebecca, nodding towards Jack.

'I'll bring some games to keep you busy, Jack. There's a garden as well.'

'Where are we going?' Jack asked again.

'Dad and I have to pack up some stuff at someone's house,' Charlie explained. 'Rebecca's going to give us a hand.'

'I can help too,' Jack told Charlie.

'It'll be boring,' said Charlie. 'Come up to my room and you can choose some games to take.'

Jack eagerly followed Charlie.

Ray came into the lounge. 'What's up with Caroline, then?' he asked Rebecca.

'She found the china head and she got really upset,' said Rebecca. It wasn't the whole story but it seemed enough to tell Ray.

'Poor woman,' said Ray. 'You two turning up must have been a real shock to her system – especially that brother of yours. Mind you, I bet she'll miss you when you go. It's like that when Charlie comes to stay – at first it's like having a herd of elephants in the place. We keep tripping over each other, can't stand each other's music and all that. Then when he goes back to his mum, the place is like a morgue – it's so quiet you can hear a pin drop, and I miss him like hell.'

Ray paused and Rebecca sensed the pain in his words. Then he smiled and changed the subject. 'You had no luck at the antiques fair, then? I told you a figurine like that would be hard to come by.'

'Do you think there's a chance we might find one today?' Rebecca asked.

'In a word – no,' said Ray.

'Maybe we shouldn't come then,' said Rebecca, instantly downhearted.

'And I thought you were that keen to help out,' Ray

teased. 'No, now you're here, you might as well come.'

They squeezed into Ray's van, Jack clutching a bag of games.

Ray drove a short distance and pulled up in front of a gated driveway. Charlie hopped out to open the gate and Ray drove through, pulling up next to a large house that looked strangely familiar.

'This house?' Rebecca stuttered.

'What about it?' said Jack.

'Don't you recognise it?' said Rebecca. 'Not even that wall?'

'What?' said Charlie. 'Is this where Jack fell? I didn't realise.'

'I don't remember,' said Jack. ' It's a high wall, isn't it? I bet you wouldn't dare climb up there, Charlie.'

'I'd have more sense,' said Charlie.

'We'd better get you inside quickly,' said Ray, taking hold of Jack's arm.

Once inside, Ray got them all organised. Jack was to sit on the sofa in the lounge and play with his games. Ray would start in the lounge too, so he could keep an eye on Jack. Charlie and Rebecca were to start upstairs, checking out the cupboards, and putting things into boxes labelled 'of interest' or 'bric-à-brac'. Any rubbish was to go into a rubbish sack.

'I won't know which is which,' Rebecca protested.

'Don't worry – you can pass each thing by me before you put it anywhere,' said Charlie, 'and Dad always checks it afterwards anyway.'

'I'm not sure . . . ' Rebecca began. She felt nervous at the idea of sorting through things that belonged to someone who had died – especially as she didn't have a clue about the difference between bric-à-brac and antiques.

Ray smiled encouragingly. 'Just do what you can – it all helps.'

Charlie led the way upstairs and Rebecca followed him into the main bedroom. The room was very pink and floral and smelt like stale perfume. Rebecca stood nervously as Charlie put down the boxes.

'If there are any china figures . . . ' she began hesitantly, 'where do you think they might be?'

'We've got to go through everything, so if there are any in the house, we'll find them,' said Charlie.

He opened the top drawer beside the bed.

'Here – this is a good place for you to start. The drawer's full of old papers – you can chuck them all into the rubbish sack.'

'Mightn't someone want them – her family...?' Rebecca asked, uneasily. She wished she could just go round the house looking for china figures, but she didn't like to suggest it.

'The woman didn't have any children, and her sister's long dead,' said Charlie. 'Dad says a distant cousin has inherited the place and he's already been round and taken everything he wanted to keep.'

'Oh.' Rebecca was wishing that she hadn't come.

Charlie opened the wardrobe and began taking things out. Rebecca pulled the shoebox of letters out of the drawer and put it on the bed. She began to flick through the letters. The woman seemed to have kept every personal letter she'd ever received. 'Dear Esme,' they all began.

Unwilling to simply push the lot of them into the rubbish sack, Rebecca began to read. The top letters weren't very interesting – clearly from one old woman to another, all about people they both knew and various ailments they were suffering from. Some of the writing was too straggly to read.

Rebecca reached deeper into the box. Among the letters there were all kinds of invitations – christenings, weddings, anniversary parties. They all dated back between ten and thirty years. If she didn't have much family, Esme clearly had a lot of friends at one time.

As she was flicking through, Rebecca was sure she'd caught a glimpse of the name 'Caroline' on one of the cards. She wondered if it was the same Caroline. It was hard to imagine their aunt throwing parties. It took a while searching to find the card. It was a white invitation with a gold rim. She pulled it out and read the writing.

She was so stunned, she had to read the words again. She must have misread it. It didn't make sense. It didn't make any sense at all.

'Marjorie Walters, together with Kenneth and Julia Grove, request the pleasure of Esme Brown's company, to celebrate the marriage of Miss Caroline Walters and Mr Neil Grove.'

'*Caroline Walters and Neil Grove*,' she repeated silently in her mind. 'But my dad's name is Neil Grove. I'm sure it is. There can't be two Neil Groves, can there? How can my aunt have married my dad? It doesn't make sense.' Nausea rose in her throat.

'When?' was the next question in her mind. She looked at the date. The wedding day was less than a year before Rebecca was born – thirteen years ago.

What did it mean?

'Are you all right?' Charlie asked, glancing round at her. 'You're supposed to be throwing them out, not reading them. We'll be here all day at this rate!' He bent down over the box he was filling, shuffling things around to make more space in it.

Rebecca felt as if her head was about to explode, with her stomach not far behind. She sat fixed to the spot, staring at the card, as if waiting for the words to change – or to start making sense.

'Becca! Becca! Get downstairs!' Jack shouted.

'What's he done now?' said Charlie, going out onto the landing.

Rebecca couldn't move. For an instant she wanted to go to Jack, but the card in her hand seemed more urgent – demanding her full attention.

'Hi, Charlie!' Jack was on the stairs. 'You'll never guess what I've found. Come and see!'

'Becca!' Jack's voice rose as he shouted up the stairs. Then she heard his footsteps going down with Charlie and was relieved. She needed time, space alone to think this through.

But when she didn't come down, Charlie came back up to find her.

'You're not going to believe . . . ' he began, but when he saw her face he stopped still.

'What's the matter?'

'Is she coming?' It was Jack's voice – he was on the stairs, and the heavier footsteps meant Ray was coming with him. They were all coming and Rebecca couldn't face them. Not now, not when she didn't understand.

'Rebecca?' Charlie spoke but his voice sounded worlds away.

'I have to get out – I need some air,' she stuttered, and pushed hard past them all and down the stairs, still holding the card.

Chapter 25

Rebecca didn't know where to go. She just ran – and found herself heading towards the river. She could hear Charlie following and she ran faster. Why couldn't he leave her be? She needed time on her own.

'Rebecca!' Charlie shouted. 'Don't run away! Tell me what's wrong.'

He was gaining on her but she kept running. She reached the river, panting for breath, trying not to slow down.

A big body suddenly loomed in front of her. She couldn't stop and crashed straight into it.

A man's voice spoke gruffly. 'Hey! Watch out! What's up with you?'

Rebecca recognised the voice. She looked up to see Bill's surprised face staring down at her. Bill – Bill who'd said Caroline was never married. But it was here – in print. Bill had lied. He'd wanted to stop her prying probably. And after what he'd said about honesty. At that moment her fury all turned on him. As he pushed her gently back, she lunged at him, pummelling at his chest with her fists, and screaming, 'You liar! You liar!'

'Hey! That's enough!' Bill tried to grasp her arms, and Rebecca felt someone else yanking at her from behind.

Charlie pulled her round to face him. 'What's got into you?' His eyes were wide with shock. 'Just calm down a minute and tell us what's going on.'

Rebecca was breathing too fast. She couldn't calm down.

'Take some deep slow breaths,' Bill suggested. 'Here – let's go and sit you on that bench over there.'

Still puffing and panting, Rebecca allowed Charlie and Bill to lead her over to the bench. 'You lied to me!' Rebecca told Bill again.

'I don't know what you're on about,' Bill protested. 'No one calls Bill a liar. Honesty's my middle name.'

Rebecca sat down and held up the invitation. 'How do you explain this then?' she demanded.

Bill took it and peered at it closely. Then he frowned.

'What is it?' asked Charlie, sitting down beside Rebecca.

Bill sighed and tutted. Charlie stood up again and leaned over him, trying to read the invitation.

Bill looked at Rebecca. He shook his head gravely as he spoke. 'I said no good would come of keeping it from you. But it wasn't for me to start telling you – you see that, don't you? I didn't lie to you though. I'm no liar.'

'You said Caroline was never married,' Rebecca reminded him.

'Yes – and that she wasn't. She never went through with it – not after what happened.'

'What do you mean?' Rebecca asked. Her head was still buzzing and she couldn't make sense of it.

Bill looked surprised that she hadn't worked it out. 'Your mother,' he began, 'she...' He stopped abruptly. 'Look, this is for your aunt to be telling you – not me. Come on – I think it's time you and she had a proper talk.'

'What about Jack – where is he?' Rebecca demanded, suddenly remembering him.

'It's okay,' Charlie assured her. 'Dad said he'd stay with him while I went after you. I'd better get back to them. They'll be wondering what on earth's happened. Is that all right – or do you want me to stay with you? I'm not sure what this is all about, but...'

'No,' said Rebecca. 'You go and make sure Jack's okay. I think I need to talk to Caroline on my own.'

'I'll see you later,' said Charlie. He gave her a bewildered look as he headed off. Rebecca walked with Bill towards Caroline's.

Bill rang the front doorbell, while Rebecca stood anxiously on the step behind him.

When Caroline opened the door and saw them, her face visibly dropped. 'It's Jack, isn't it?' she said fearfully. 'What's happened to him now?'

Bill shifted uncomfortably. 'No, Caroline, it's not Jack. It's this young lady here.'

Caroline looked at Rebecca. 'You do look a mess, Rebecca. What's going on? Where's Jack?'

'Jack's with Ray – Charlie's dad,' Rebecca whispered.

'And?' Caroline asked.

Rebecca opened her mouth but nothing more came out.

'I'm sorry, Caroline, but she knows,' Bill said solemnly. 'She knows about you and Neil. And before you start – it wasn't my doing. I haven't said a thing.' He held the invitation card out to Caroline. 'She found this. Don't ask me how or where. But you'll have to talk to her now. If you ask me, it's for the best. She was bound to find out sooner or later.'

Caroline read the card and then stood, head bowed, eyes closed, as if she was trying to pretend none of it was happening.

'I'll leave you to have a talk then,' Bill said, hovering uncertainly on the doorstep.

Caroline didn't speak, so Bill gave Rebecca an encouraging wink and walked away.

Rebecca shuffled awkwardly inside. Caroline finally joined her, moving as if in slow motion. The front door banged closed. Caroline led the way to the kitchen.

'I'll put the kettle on,' she said flatly.

They sat down opposite each other. At first neither of them spoke.

Finally Caroline dropped the invitation on the table. 'Where did you get this?' she asked, sighing.

'We were helping Ray and Charlie with a house clearance,' Rebecca explained. 'It was that house – the one where Jack had his fall – but I didn't know that was where we were going until we got there. Anyway, you never said you knew who lived there.'

'Esme?' said Caroline. Her voice softened. 'Yes – she was a dear friend of my grandmother – and she was very good to my parents too, and me. Ninety-six, she was when she died. I went to her funeral last month. When Jack fell off that wall it didn't seem very relevant to mention it.'

She stood up stiffly to pour the drinks. 'Tea?' she asked.

Rebecca nodded. 'Charlie said I should go through one of the drawers and throw out all the papers,' she explained. 'Only, I started looking through them. I couldn't help it. And I saw your name. I want you to tell me everything – please, Caroline. I want to know what happened.'

Caroline put the cups of tea on the table and sat down, meeting Rebecca's eyes with a grave expression.

'I can see how upset you are already,' she said doubtfully. 'I knew it would be better for you not to know. That was one thing your mother and I agreed about.'

Rebecca gave her an angry stare. 'I think I have a right. It's my family too.'

Caroline's shoulders sank and she leant back in the chair, sighing. 'Maybe it's best if you ask me what you want to know,' she said, folding her arms.

'You were engaged to Neil, right?' Rebecca began.

Caroline nodded.

'And he's my dad?'

Caroline nodded again.

'And in the end you never married him?'

'That's right,' said Caroline.

'Because of Mum?' Rebecca asked.

'Yes.'

'So,' Rebecca said, heaving with tension. 'What exactly did Mum do?'

Caroline's eyes half closed as if in pain, and then opened again. 'She ran off with Neil – a week before we were supposed to be married.'

'My mum ran off with your fiancé?' said Rebecca. It couldn't be true. It sounded impossible.

Caroline nodded.

'But why? I mean how? How could she do a thing like that?'

'That you'll have to ask her, I'm afraid,' Caroline said bitterly. 'All I can tell you is that I was in love – more in love than I'd ever been. I was always a shy girl, you see, not like your mother. But when I met Neil, I knew he was the one. He made me happy. I wanted to spend the rest of my life with him. Your mum had come up from London a few weeks before the wedding. It wasn't the first time she'd met Neil, and I was pleased that they got on well together.'

'So what happened?' Rebecca asked impatiently.

'As far as I was concerned everything was fine,' Caroline continued, 'until one day I went down to our beach hut and found them at it. Yes – Steph and Neil, my sister and my fiancé – together, eight days before our wedding. You can imagine how I felt.'

Rebecca clasped her hands round her mug of tea. So that was where the beach hut fitted in – it was all beginning to make sense, but she still didn't want to believe it. 'Mum . . .' she whispered. 'But Mum wouldn't do that . . . she couldn't. She's not like that.'

'I'd have said the same,' Caroline agreed. 'Before.

It might be hard to believe – but she *did* it all right. I should have seen the signs. I thought she was just being friendly towards Neil but after I'd found them like that, I realised all the time she'd been flirting and leading him on. I was hysterical, inconsolable. But even so, I thought Neil would come pleading – promising me it was only a meaningless slip. But he never came. And then the next day he and your mother were both missing. They'd run off together. She'd stolen him from me.'

Caroline skin tautened over her face and her lips shuddered. 'I don't think I've ever stopped waiting – hoping he would come back to me. But I never saw him again, or your mother, for that matter, from that day to this. I heard on the grapevine that she was pregnant. That was the last news I had until the phone call that brought you here.'

'How could she?' Rebecca said in disbelief. 'How could Mum do it?'

Caroline opened her mouth to speak, but at that moment the phone rang, and she hurried off to answer it.

Rebecca listened, and heard Caroline's surprised voice saying, 'Oh – Steph, it's you.'

Rebecca was so startled, the cup tipped in her hand and tea spilt out onto the table. *Mum was on the phone*. Mum. Fuelled by a sudden rage, Rebecca jumped up and ran out into the hall. She grabbed the phone before Caroline had time to say anymore.

'I know everything, Mum!' she yelled down the phone. 'I know what a bitch you are and a slag. How could you do it, Mum? Your own sister... I hate you! I hate you! I don't care if you never get off the drugs. It's what you deserve. I never want to see you or speak to you again!'

'Stop that, Rebecca!' Caroline pleaded, trying to grasp the receiver.

Caroline finally took hold of the phone and Rebecca stormed up the stairs to her room, floods of tears pouring down her face.

'Steph, Steph! Calm down,' Rebecca heard Caroline pleading. ' I didn't tell her, I promise you – don't start on me!'

Chapter 26

Rebecca lay sobbing on her bed. She had no idea how long she'd been there, and she was crying too much to hear Jack come into the house. She only knew he was back when he burst into the bedroom, demanding, 'Becca! Why did you go off like that?'

Rebecca rolled over so that she was facing away from him. Jack pulled at her shoulder.

'Go away, Jack,' she mumbled.

'Charlie just brought me back,' Jack said, leaping round to the other side of the bed. 'He wanted to come in and see you but Caroline said he better not.'

Rebecca lay still, her eyes closed. She felt exhausted. She couldn't take Jack at the moment. If anything, she'd rather have talked to Charlie.

'Go away, will you?' she said. 'I need some peace.'

'Caroline's in a right state,' Jack continued, ignoring her plea. 'Is she still upset about last night?'

'Last night?' Rebecca tried to think. Last night seemed so long ago. Finally, it came back to her. The bathroom – the china head. The whole chain of events played like a film before her closed eyes. If only – if only Jack hadn't taken that figurine and broken it in the first place, they'd never have been trying to replace it. Then she wouldn't even have been at that house clearance – and wouldn't have found the invitation. Then she wouldn't know what she knew. And Caroline was right, Rebecca thought now. She wished, more than anything, that she didn't know. She opened her eyes and the tears came once more.

'Are you still upset about it too, Becca?' Jack asked, a bewildered look on his face. ''Cos you don't need to be – not anymore.' His face was suddenly alight – with a grin almost as big as Charlie's.

'What are you on about?' Rebecca asked.

'Why we went there,' said Jack, 'you know – to that house. It's all sorted. I found one!'

'Found what?'

Jack went to the door and looked out furtively, before closing it tightly. 'In case she's nosing about,' he explained. He came back to the bed, his face beaming with excitement.

'I found it,' he told her, 'one of those china ladies – like Caroline's! Only it's not exactly the same – it's a bit the same and a bit different. You should've stayed and seen it! I wanted to bring it and show you but Ray's got it now. You'll have to wait till tomorrow.'

Rebecca pulled herself up on her pillow and rubbed her eyes. 'Say that again, Jack,' she asked him.

Jack breathed loudly in frustration. 'Are you thick or something? I'm telling you, I found a china lady like Caroline's. It was in one of those cupboards downstairs, only it was right at the back. She's gonna love it, Ray reckons. That'll cheer her up, won't it, Becca?'

'That's not why she's upset – or me,' said Rebecca, 'not right now anyway.'

Jack's smile disappeared. He frowned. 'What d'you mean?'

'I found out why she and Mum never talked for all those years,' said Rebecca.

'Really? Tell me then.'

'It's like this. Caroline was engaged to marry my dad – Neil. Then Mum ran off with him.'

'I don't get it,' said Jack.

Rebecca didn't feel like explaining. 'Look – why don't you go away and leave me alone for a bit. I'll tell you about it later.'

'But, Becca – aren't you pleased about the china lady?' Jack demanded, his voice rising into a whine.

'Yes, it's great,' she said, but her voice was lifeless. She wanted to share Jack's excitement about it, but somehow a figurine for Caroline seemed the least important thing right now.

'You wait till you see it,' Jack said stubbornly.

He left the room and Rebecca suddenly felt very alone. She cried some more and then finally slept.

She woke to find Caroline leaning over her, her eyes red and puffy. Rebecca clearly wasn't the only one who'd been crying.

'I thought you might want something to eat,' said Caroline. 'I've put the tray on the bedside table. There's a glass of orange juice too. Shall I open the window? It's ever so hot in here.'

She didn't wait for a reply but went straight over to the window. 'You should never have spoken to your mother like that,' she said grimly, as she pulled at the catch.

'I hate her,' Rebecca retorted. 'I hate her for what she did. And you hate her too, don't you?'

Caroline said nothing. A gust of wind ruffled her hair

as she turned back to face Rebecca. Apart from her red eyes, her face looked grey. There was a long silence.

'Did you never meet anyone else, after Neil?' Rebecca asked, curiously.

'No. He was the only one,' said Caroline.

'What about Bill?' said Rebecca.

'Bill?' Caroline exclaimed, open-mouthed. 'Where did you get that idea? No – I had no eyes for anyone but Neil. Now, I'd better go and check on Jack. Charlie left him some of those electronic games to play with – and they seemed to be keeping him occupied – but you never know with Jack. . . '

Caroline left the room quickly. She clearly didn't want to talk about it anymore. Poor Caroline, Rebecca thought. After what Mum had done, it was incredibly kind of her to have them to stay. Caroline's words from the night before suddenly came back to her, filling her with guilt. '*Nothing but trouble*' the two of them had brought, and now Rebecca had churned up the past, bringing Caroline even more pain. She wished she could do something to make it up to her – but what could she do?

Then she remembered what Jack had said – that he'd found a figurine like Caroline's. He'd said she would love it – even Ray thought so. It couldn't make up for all of this, but maybe it could go some way to showing Caroline that she and Jack weren't all bad – unlike *Mum*.

Chapter 27

The next morning Jack woke Rebecca early.

'Come on! Get up, Becca! I want to go round to Charlie's so you can see it.'

'See what?'

'The china lady for Caroline,' Jack whispered, screwing up his face in exasperation. 'The one I found.'

'All right, Jack. I'll be up in a minute.'

At breakfast, Jack's energy and cheerful mood was a dramatic contrast with her own, and Caroline's.

'Sit still, Jack!' Caroline snapped.

'I'll take him out this morning and give you some peace,' Rebecca told Caroline. She nodded gratefully.

Jack bounded along the road towards the antique shop, and Rebecca had a job to keep up with him.

'Slow down, Jack,' she panted.

As they reached the shop, Charlie came out to greet them.

'Are you all right?' he asked Rebecca. 'I wanted to talk to you yesterday – make sure you were okay, but Caroline...'

'I know,' Rebecca said, nodding. 'I'll tell you about it all later.'

'How's Caroline?' Ray asked, as they joined him inside. 'Do you think she's ready for this surprise?'

'She'll go mad over it!' said Jack.

Ray took one look at Jack's excited state and suggested they go into the back room. They stood round as Ray carefully unwound the tissue paper from the figurine, and held it out for Rebecca to see.

Rebecca gasped. She hadn't imagined anything as beautiful as this. The figure was the same size as the one that had been broken, and was painted in the same delicate way. The dress and face were different though. The head tilted up and had a happy, carefree expression.

Rebecca met Ray's eyes briefly and he smiled.

'Well?' said Jack, impatiently. 'What d'you think?'

'It's lovely,' said Rebecca. 'But we can't give it to Caroline.'

'Why not?' Jack demanded, in surprise.

'We don't have the money to pay for it,' said Rebecca.

'But Ray said he'd pay for it if we found one, didn't you, Ray?'

'But he didn't think we *could* find one,' Rebecca pointed out. 'And we couldn't let him pay for it anyway.'

'But I don't have to pay for it, do I?' Ray pointed out. 'I agreed a price with Esme's cousin for the total house contents, so the figurine is mine. And that wasn't the only thing Jack found at the back of that cabinet. There were a few other good pieces too. I'll make a fair bit out of it all. Jack did well, even if he wasn't supposed to be poking about.' He gave Jack a wry smile.

'This one's not as rare as the one that was broken,' he continued, 'but it's a fine piece all the same. There was a catalogue in the cabinet with it, showing that Esme bought it at an auction at a stately home down the road, about fifteen years ago. And would you believe it, that figure of Caroline's was in the same sale. That must have been when she bought it. Anyway, I'd be delighted for Caroline to have it.'

'Are you sure?' Rebecca looked at him questioningly. It was very generous of him.

'Yes – I'm sure. I'll find a good box for it and I think I've got some wrapping paper somewhere and you can give it to her today.'

'We'll tell her *I* found it, won't we?' Jack demanded.

'Yes, we'll tell her,' said Rebecca.

Ray found a box exactly the right size. He re-wrapped the figurine carefully in tissue paper. Charlie fetched some sellotape and scissors, and Rebecca carefully wrapped the box.

'Will you come with us when we give it to her?' Jack asked Charlie.

Charlie looked unsure.

'Yes,' said Rebecca. 'We'd never have found it without your help, and Ray of course.'

'I can't leave the shop, I'm afraid,' said Ray. 'But you go, Charlie, if you want.'

'I'll carry it!' said Jack.

'I don't think so,' said Rebecca.

Jack pouted.

'Why don't we let Charlie carry it?' Rebecca suggested quickly.

Jack's face lit up. 'Yeh – you carry it, Charlie. But you better not drop it!'

Chapter 28

They left the shop and walked to Caroline's. She did not look pleased to see them back so soon.

'We've got a present for you!' Jack told her excitedly.

Caroline looked stunned. 'A present? What's that in aid of?'

'It's . . . ' Rebecca thought for a moment. 'It's to thank you for having us here.'

Caroline frowned, doubtfully. 'You'd better come in then.'

She led them through to the kitchen. Charlie placed the present on the table.

Jack bounced up and down. 'Go on – open it, Caroline!'

Caroline looked at the present suspiciously. 'This isn't a trick, is it? I'm not going to get covered with exploding streamers when I open it, am I?'

'No,' Rebecca assured her. 'It's a real present.'

Caroline began to fumble with the sellotape, pulling it off carefully strip by strip. 'It's lovely paper,' she commented. 'It would be a shame to scrunch it up and throw it away. I'm sure it could be re-used.'

Jack huffed impatiently. Charlie met Rebecca's eyes and grinned.

Finally, Caroline had the paper off. She opened the lid of the box, and began to unravel the tissue paper. Her hands froze as she revealed the figurine. She stared at it in disbelief.

'Don't you like it?' Jack asked. He'd clearly expected more enthusiasm.

'Where did you get this?' Caroline demanded.

'We've been looking for one ever since that one of yours got broken,' Rebecca explained.

'And I found this one!' said Jack.

'This is not the kind of thing you find lying around,' Caroline said sternly. 'And there's no way you can possibly have paid for it.' She looked aghast. 'I was just beginning to think the two of you . . . But now – *stealing*! You, Charlie, you're old enough to know better.'

'But you've got it all wrong,' said Charlie. 'Dad helped them out. They found it at the house clearance and he said they could have it, to give you. Honestly – that's what happened.'

'And why should he do a thing like that?' Caroline asked, clearly not believing a word she was hearing.

'It's a present. Why are you so angry?' Jack asked, his eyes wide and indignant.

'I expect we'll have the police round here next,' said Caroline. 'I don't think I can take anymore.' She leaned weakly against the kitchen worktop, and Rebecca saw that her hands were shaking.

'Please!' Charlie begged. 'Let me go and get Dad – he'll come and tell you it's the truth.'

Before Caroline could respond, Charlie was out in the hallway, and they heard the front door bang behind him.

Jack stormed off through the kitchen and out the back

door, and Rebecca chased after him, anxious about what he would do.

'She doesn't even like it, Becca,' he moaned, flinging himself down on the grass.

'I think she will,' Rebecca assured him, 'once Ray explains how we got it. It must seem dodgy, mustn't it, Jack? It'll be all right when Ray gets here. Let's go back in.'

It seemed like an age before Ray arrived. Rebecca showed him into the kitchen and he stood awkwardly, looking at Caroline. He cleared his throat.

'I can't be long – I've had to shut the shop. Charlie says you think this figure's been *stolen*? It's my fault – I should have thought. Anyway, I can promise you, they definitely didn't steal it. They came into the shop, asking for my help to find a replacement for one of yours that had been broken. They had no idea what it was worth, of course.'

Rebecca watched Caroline's face, as Ray spoke. She was listening but her expression wasn't changing.

'When I told them how rare it was,' Ray continued, 'they were most upset. Charlie here was determined to help them try and find one, but I thought it was a hopeless task. That was why they'd come to help with the house clearance. Rebecca here wanted to take every chance of finding one. We weren't expecting Jack, and I'll admit, I was trying to keep his fingers out of everything. But he came up trumps with a small escapade into the back of a cabinet. Out he came, with this in his hand. I thought they deserved to have it – to give to you.'

Caroline looked amazed. 'Is . . . is all that true?'

She turned to Rebecca, Jack and then Charlie.

They all nodded.

'Then I'm sorry. It's been a stressful time – but I know that's no excuse. I can't believe you went to all that trouble.' She picked up the figurine and stroked it affectionately.

She turned to Ray. 'You must let me pay for it though. I can't possibly keep it otherwise.'

'I won't hear of it,' Ray said forcefully, to Rebecca's relief. He explained about the other things Jack had found. 'So you see, I'll make a fair bit on those.'

'But . . . ' Caroline began.

Ray shook his head.

Caroline looked from him to the figurine and back again, then at Rebecca and Jack. 'Nothing can replace my Arabella, but this is a beautiful piece. I will treasure it. Thank you.'

To Rebecca's surprise, Caroline bent down and kissed Jack, and then her.

Then she shook Charlie's hand, and then Ray's. 'Thank you both too.'

'I must get back to the shop,' said Ray, 'but before I go – I have a day off tomorrow, my friend Barry's minding the shop. I was thinking about taking Charlie to Framlingham Castle. I wondered if the three of you would like to join us? We could take a picnic . . . '

Jack's eyes widened in excitement. 'A castle? I've never been to a real castle! Say we can, Caroline! Please!'

'That's very kind of you,' Caroline told Ray. 'Take the

children, by all means, but I'm afraid I have too much work to do.'

'Please come, Caroline,' said Rebecca. 'It would be lovely to all be out together.'

'It would be more eyes to watch Jack with, if you came,' Ray said, cocking his head slightly on one side.

'You have a point there,' said Caroline. 'It'd be unfair of me to leave you to keep hold of him – especially at a castle.'

'You'll come then?' Ray asked.

'Yes – I'll come,' said Caroline.

Chapter 29

Caroline busied herself in the afternoon, making a shopping list and heading off to the supermarket to buy food for a picnic to take to the castle. Charlie offered to take Rebecca and Jack crabbing. Rebecca was pleased, as she wanted a chance to talk things through with him. It meant having Jack with them, but there didn't seem any way out of that.

'It's the crabbing competition next weekend,' Charlie told them. 'If you're going to stand a chance, you'll have to get some practice in.'

Charlie sorted them out with lines and bait, and they took the ferry over to Walberswick. They found a good place on the bridge over the creek, and set to work. Rebecca feared Jack wouldn't sit still for even five minutes, but it was something new and he surprised her by sitting rigidly, waiting for the slightest pull on his line. Rebecca began to talk to Charlie, explaining about the invitation and what Mum had done.

'I hate her now,' she told Charlie. 'I don't care if I never see her again.'

'I do,' Jack protested. 'I want to see Mum. I wish we could see her today.'

'Well, I don't,' said Rebecca.

'It can't all have been your mum's fault, though,

can it?' said Charlie. 'I mean, it takes two to tango, as Dad would say. Neil's the baddie if you ask me. He dumped Caroline and went off with your mum, didn't he?'

'I suppose.'

'He's right, Becca,' said Jack. 'And Mum always said your dad was a bad piece of work – you told me that. He left Mum when she was pregnant with you, didn't he?'

'He'd probably never have been a good husband to Caroline, anyway,' Charlie pointed out. 'Not if he's the kind of man who could behave like that.'

'If my mum and dad are both rotten pigs,' Rebecca said bitterly, 'then what does that make me?'

'You're your own person,' said Charlie. 'You can be whatever you want to be.'

'Mum's not a rotten pig anyway,' Jack protested.

'I wish none of it had ever happened,' said Rebecca, trying to hold back the tears.

'Then you wouldn't have been born, would you?' Charlie pointed out. 'And if you ask me, that would be a big shame – a really big shame.' He met Rebecca's eyes and she blushed.

Jack made as if he was going to throw up. 'Yuck. He'll be kissing you next.'

'Will you shut up?' said Rebecca. But she could feel she was blushing even more.

'Charlie! Charlie!' Jack cried. 'I think I've got one! Something's pulling on my line!'

'Keep still,' Charlie warned him, 'and reel it in very gently.'

Jack couldn't keep still so Charlie gave him a hand to reel in the line. At last the top of the bait appeared, followed by a small crab, who was clinging on tightly.

'I caught one, Charlie!' Jack cried ecstatically.

'Well done,' said Charlie. 'But you'll have to catch a bigger one than that to win the competition.'

'I will!' said Jack. 'I'll catch the hugest, whoppingest crab you've ever seen. You wait!'

Later, when they'd said goodbye to Charlie, and were walking back to Caroline's, Rebecca found she was beginning to worry about Mum, and the things she'd said to her.

'I want to speak to Mum,' she told Caroline, as soon as they were inside.

'So do I,' Jack piped up.

'I'll phone for you,' said Caroline, 'but it may not be convenient for your mum to speak, so bear that in mind.'

Rebecca waited anxiously as Caroline made the call.

'Here,' said Caroline, holding the phone out to Rebecca. 'They're putting it through to your mum now. I'm afraid I don't feel like talking to her at the moment.'

'Mum?' said Rebecca.

'Oh, Rebecca, love – I'm so glad to speak to you.' Mum spoke fast and sounded breathless. Her voice made Rebecca instantly anxious.

'Mum – is it going okay there?' Rebecca was scared now, scared that her outburst might have messed up Mum's chances of getting clean.

'It's hard,' said Mum. 'Sometimes I think it's impossible. But I will do it, love. We're going to the cinema tomorrow.'

Rebecca was stunned. 'The cinema?'

'Yes – it's not a prison, you know. It's not even like a hospital. It's more like a big house. We can go out, as long as someone comes with us to make sure we don't do anything naughty. So it's not that bad.'

It didn't sound at all as bad as Rebecca had imagined and she was relieved. If Mum was going to the cinema, then they must think she was doing okay.

'Mum . . . ' Rebecca said awkwardly, 'I'm sorry for what I said yesterday – I didn't mean to call you all those things. It was a shock, that's all.'

'It must've been.'

There was a pause, and then a long sigh from Mum. 'I didn't want you finding out like that. I thought Caroline agreed with me.'

'It wasn't her fault.' Rebecca explained about meeting Charlie and helping out with the house clearance. She heard Mum gasp when she came to the bit about the invitation.

'What a way to find out,' she exclaimed.

'Why did you do it, Mum?' Rebecca asked.

'Oh, Rebecca. It's hard to explain now. I know it's no excuse, but I was young – nineteen, and I got a bit caught up with all the attention Neil kept paying me. He was dead good looking, and as far as I was concerned it was only a bit of fun, flirting and that. Then I suppose we got a bit carried away. And when Caroline caught us . . . it was a terrible mess. I couldn't believe what I'd done. I was petrified of how my mum was going to react. I felt so ashamed.'

'You didn't have to run off with him though, did you?' said Rebecca.

'That wasn't my idea,' Mum told her. 'I thought Neil would either leave quickly, or stay and try and sort things out. I was shocked when he said we should run off together. I don't know why I went along with him. It was an easy option, I suppose, running away – and I was flattered that he wanted to stay with me. I thought I was in love, too. Then, once we'd gone – it was like, there was no turning back.'

'So you pretended you never had a sister?' Rebecca asked. 'I don't know how you could do that.'

'It was all I *could* do, to cope with the guilt. I tried to push Caroline out of my mind completely – I knew she and my mum would never forgive me. I was pretty miserable, I'm telling you. And Neil wasn't such a great catch as it turned out. Once I was pregnant with you, he scarpered. I was on my own in London. I had no family, no job – nothing. You're the only good thing that came out of any of it, Rebecca. Just you.'

'Oh, Mum.'

'I was a mess, Rebecca, and it was hard being on my own with a baby – even though I loved you to bits. Where I was living, people around me were all taking stuff – to help them get by.'

'Drugs, you mean?' said Rebecca. 'But I thought it was Mitch that got you started in all that.'

Mum hesitated. 'It wasn't just Mitch. Before I met Gary – that was when it first started – when you were a baby. I know you must think I'm awful. I've been a terrible mother to you. You must hate me and I don't blame you.'

'I don't hate you, Mum,' said Rebecca. 'I just don't understand why you did it.'

'Nor do I,' said Mum. 'I was dead against drugs to start with, but then I thought why not? Just now and then wouldn't do any harm.

'If I hadn't met Gary I'd probably have got hooked back then. He set me straight – he was shocked that I was being so irresponsible, when I had a baby to look after. He said he'd look after us both – but I had to stop the drugs. And I did stop. Gary made me feel like I was worth something. We moved into that house and I thought he really loved me. I got a part-time job and then I had Jack. We were happy, weren't we? I wasn't to know he was going to up and leave us like that – make us homeless.

'You know how it was after that. I was so stressed out. I met Mitch and we got on really well. He had some heroin. He gave me a cut – and it made me feel so relaxed – it was like all my worries went away. And I knew I'd been able to stop before – so I never thought I'd get hooked. I wouldn't have done it if I'd thought that. But you feel so good when you've taken it, that as soon as you come back down to earth you want more – and then gradually you find you need more and more of it to keep feeling the same. All the time I thought I was in control – but now I realise it had taken me over. I just didn't see it.

'I was talking about it this morning with one of the

therapists here. She said it was probably the best thing that this has all come out now – about Caroline and Neil and everything. She thinks when I got into drugs – part of it was about trying to escape from the guilt of what I did. She says I'll have much more chance of keeping clean, now it's out in the open and I can deal with it. I suppose I've got you to thank for that.'

'Me?' It hadn't occurred to Rebecca that Mum's drug problem could have anything to do with all this.

'That's why I've decided to come up and fetch you myself, when I finish here. If Caroline agrees, of course. It's time she and I had a talk. I want to sort things out with her if I can.'

'Really?' This was the last thing Rebecca had expected.

'Yes. Can you put me on to Caroline?' Mum asked. 'No – actually I'd better speak to Jack first or I'll be for it, won't I?'

Rebecca called Jack to the phone, and went into the kitchen to talk to Caroline.

'Mum says she wants to come here when she's finished at the clinic – and sort things out with you. You will let her, won't you?' Rebecca's voice rose pleadingly.

Caroline looked startled. Her eyes narrowed. 'Come here? No, I don't think that's a good idea at all. Too much has happened, Rebecca. We can't start playing happy families after all this time.'

'I think Mum wants to make it up with you,' said Rebecca. 'I know she's sorry for what she did. At least speak to her on the phone.'

'And she'll come here and expcct me to forgive her just like that? No – it's not on and that's final.' Caroline pursed her lips.

Jack called Caroline to the phone but she didn't move.

Rebccca went and took the phone from Jack. 'It's no good, Mum,' she said. 'Caroline won't talk to you. I tried my best to persuade her.'

'Don't worry, love,' said Mum, but she sounded deeply disappointed.

Chapter 30

The trip to Framlingham Castle the next day was excellent. Jack loved every minute, and with Charlie, Caroline and Ray, the strain of watching him wasn't all on Rebecca's shoulders. Caroline looked happier and more relaxed than Rebecca had seen her since they arrived, and she and Ray seemed to enjoy each other's company.

Rebecca enjoyed being with Charlie. She had even grown to like his grin. He was quite good looking really – especially those big greeny-blue eyes. Her favourite part of the trip was the picnic. Sitting on rugs, eating chicken legs and crisps and laughing together, she was reminded of those families she and Jack had seen picnicking on the green. Now they looked just the same – and even though they weren't really a family, it was a good feeling.

In the evening Jack came into Rebecca's room.

'That was my best day ever,' he said, throwing himself onto her bed.

Rebecca smiled. 'It was good, wasn't it?'

'Is Charlie your boyfriend now?' Jack asked.

'No, of course not,' Rebecca said quickly.

'I think he is,' said Jack.

Rebecca wasn't sure what to say, but to her relief, Jack changed the subject.

'You'll never guess what I saw Caroline doing just now.'

'What?' asked Rebecca.

'She was burying that china head – in the garden.'

'Burying it?' Rebecca repeated.

'Yeh – I was getting a drink in the kitchen and I looked out of the window and saw her. She was in the garden, burying it. She didn't see me watching – but I know that's what she was doing. She'd dug a hole and she was holding the head – I saw it.'

'Why would she bury it?' Rebecca asked, more to herself than to Jack.

'I reckon she must've known it had special powers,' said Jack. 'Otherwise why didn't she just throw it away?'

Rebecca wasn't sure, and didn't reply. Somehow now it sounded silly – the idea of a china head having 'special powers'. It was hard to believe it could really have been responsible for everything from the scratch on the bedside chest to Jack's fall. Even so, she was secretly glad to hear Caroline had buried it. It felt like the right thing to do.

'And now I found her a new one she doesn't need that old head anymore,' said Jack. 'She looked well-happy today, didn't she?'

Rebecca nodded. Caroline had looked happy.

'It's because of the china lady,' said Jack. 'That broken head was making all bad things happen, and now I found her a new one, all good things are happening, aren't they? Caroline's happy and we got to go to a castle . . . '

'I don't believe that head made anything happen really,' said Rebecca. 'I think it just seemed like it was. Those things must have been coincidences, that's all.'

'But it was angry when it got broken, and then it was making us get her another one – it was trying to show us – that's why it made me fall in that garden – it knew there was one in that house. That's what I think, anyway.'

Rebecca found the dreams coming back into her mind. It had seemed like the china figures were trying to get her to do something. But dreams were only dreams. Ornaments were just ornaments. They had no minds, no brains. They couldn't make holes appear in drawers, or washing machines stop working, or shelves crack, or hands hurt, or people fall.

'I think it's rubbish, Jack.'

'It's not!'

'It is!'

'It's not!'

Jack picked up a pillow and thumped Rebecca with it. She grabbed it and thumped him back. They were rolling around giggling, when Caroline came into the room.

'Time for bed, Jack, I think,' Caroline told him.

'Can I ask you something?' Rebecca said to Caroline. She sat up and pointed to the scratch on the bedside table. 'You see this scratch? I'm not sure if it was there before or if Jack or I might have done it by accident.'

'That?' Caroline said, coming to inspect it. 'Oh – that scratch has been there for years. I remember my mother being angry when she found it after one of the guests had left. I've no idea how it happened. So you can relax. It certainly wasn't your fault.'

As Caroline left the room, Rebecca gave Jack a 'told you so' look. 'See! The head didn't do that, so I bet it didn't do anything else either.'

'That's only one thing,' Jack pointed out, sticking his tongue out back to her. 'I know it did the other things, so there.'

'Believe what you like,' said Rebecca, shrugging.

It took about an hour before Jack was actually settled in bed. The castle has over-excited him and he refused to go to sleep.

When Rebecca went up to the bathroom to get ready for bed herself, she heard noises coming from the room where Jack had found the dresses in the wardrobe.

'What's he doing in there?' she muttered to herself, crossly. She pushed the door open and was surprised to see not Jack, but Caroline in the room.

Caroline had all the dresses out, and was wrapping them and putting them in bags. She looked up.

'Sorry – I thought you were Jack,' Rebecca stuttered.

'Don't worry,' Caroline said cheerfully.

Rebecca saw uncomfortably that the wedding dress was already wrapped and poking out of one of the bags.

'I was looking for a dress,' Caroline explained, 'but I think these are all well past it. I've decided to treat myself to a new one.'

'Is it for something special?' Rebecca asked curiously. The dresses looked too smart to wear casually.

Caroline blushed. 'Ray has invited me out to dinner tomorrow night. I'll need something special to wear. I was wondering – how would you feel about coming with me tomorrow to help me choose a new dress? It's a long time since I've had anything to dress up for...'

'Of course I will,' said Rebecca.

*

With her new dress, new hairstyle and make-up and new shoes, Caroline looked years younger and much prettier. She even seemed to hold her head higher.

In the days that followed, Ray and Caroline spent quite a bit of time together. Everything seemed different and Rebecca began to feel as if she was really on holiday. A funfair arrived on the common, and she went with Jack and Charlie. Caroline had given her pocket money so Rebecca was able to pay Charlie back and treat him to an ice-cream or two as well. The weather was good and they spent lots of time on the beach and by the river, where they continued practising for the crabbing competition.

The competition itself was like nothing Rebecca had ever seen. There were hundreds of people; adults and children, all lined up along the creek with their lines, buckets and bait – usually either fish skeletons or bacon. A gun was fired to mark the start, and gentle music played while everyone waited for a pull on their line.

Jack – after managing not to fall in during all their practice runs, got so excited when he landed a big crab, that he tripped over the line and went flying into the creek.

Luckily there was a man in a boat in the creek, who was there to retrieve any 'windfalls' and Jack was quickly rescued. He enjoyed all the attention until he discovered that anyone who falls in is automatically disqualified.

'But my crab's a whoppa!' he kept insisting.

'You're soaked, Jack,' said Rebecca, standing back to stop him dripping all over her. 'We'll have to take you back to Caroline's to change.'

'It's sunny – I'll soon dry,' said Jack.

'But you can't win now anyway,' Rebecca reminded him.

Reluctantly, Jack allowed Ray to give him a lift back to Caroline's, wrapped in a towel that someone had lent him. They soon returned, with Jack in dry clothes and Caroline with them. By this time Charlie had landed three crabs, though none of them was as big as Jack's.

'Put mine in your bucket,' Jack told him. 'No one will know – then you can win, but it will really be me.'

'I'm not cheating,' said Charlie, grinning.

'I should hope not,' said Caroline.

Jack paced up and down in frustration. 'I wanted to win,' he moaned.

In the end, the judges allowed Jack's crab to be weighed, and discovered that it was actually the largest. They couldn't award him first prize because he had been disqualified, but they relented and awarded him a 'booby' prize of a T-shirt that said, 'I caught crabs at Walberswick'. Jack was delighted.

As they walked away from the river, Rebecca became aware of just how attached she was beginning to feel to the place. She wished they never had to leave.

'There's something I think I ought to tell you,' Caroline said to Rebecca when they had a brief moment alone, that evening.

'What is it?' Rebecca asked, looking worried.

'Tomorrow your mother's having an assessment. It's to see if they think she's well enough to look after you. There is a small possibility that they might decide she needs a longer rehabilitation programme.'

'But what about us?' Rebecca demanded.

'Let's wait and see, shall we?' said Caroline. 'I just thought you ought to know.'

Rebecca waited anxiously for the call from Mum with the result of her assessment. When the phone rang she ran to pick it up.

'Mum! How did it go?' she asked.

'They said I've done really well,' said Mum. 'They'd have liked me to go on to a rehab. centre for a few months, but there's a heck of a waiting list, and there's you two to consider, of course. So they've decided it'll be okay for us all to go home. How about that?'

Rebecca heaved a huge sigh of relief. 'That's great, Mum.'

'I know it's not going to be easy, but I'll have the social worker and I'll go to some sessions at the centre to help me get back on my feet. I hope I'll soon be able to get a new job. Listen, do you think Caroline might speak to me now? Tell her I want to thank her for having you both – perhaps that'll do the trick.'

Rebecca called Caroline. 'Please speak to Mum. She only wants to thank you for having us,' Rebecca pleaded.

Caroline hesitated a long time. But she finally took the phone. Rebecca stood waiting to hear what she'd say but Caroline waved her arm and made faces indicating that Rebecca should go away.

Rebecca waited in the kitchen. When Caroline joined her Rebecca thought she was looking quite shaky.

'What happened?' she asked.

'It's a beginning,' Caroline mumbled. 'I've said she

can come and pick you up tomorrow. We'll talk more then.'

'Brilliant!' said Rebecca.

'I've been doing a lot of thinking,' said Caroline. 'You know, I always imagined your mother was having a great time with Neil, especially after I heard she was pregnant – having his child. I felt bitter thinking she had all the happiness that should have been mine.'

'But she hasn't been happy,' said Rebecca.

'I know – it was Jack who put me right on that – told me Neil had left your mum in the lurch, and that his own father had left too. I didn't know you had different fathers until then. And your mum's had the drug problem as well.'

Caroline paused. She looked anxious. 'It's not going to be easy to talk about what happened after all this time.'

'At least you're going to try,' said Rebecca. 'Mum is sorry – I know she is.'

That night as she lay in bed, Rebecca's mind churned. She couldn't wait to see Mum but the thought of leaving this place and going back to that miserable flat was depressing. Suddenly she had an idea. Caroline had loads of spare rooms. If Caroline made up with Mum then why couldn't they all move in here with her? As she thought about it, the idea had more and more appeal. Living by the sea would be wonderful for Jack – and Mum would be far less likely to go back on the drugs. Rebecca couldn't imagine any drug dealers in a place like this.

She couldn't wait to suggest it to Caroline.

Chapter 31

It was their last day.

'How about a walk on the beach and then you can finish off the packing?' Caroline suggested. 'We've got time before your mum arrives.'

'Can I fly my kite?' Jack asked. 'Charlie gave it to me. He showed me how to fly it.'

Caroline smiled. 'Yes, of course you can.'

It was windy on the beach. Rebecca held the kite while Jack ran ahead with the string.

'Let go when I say,' he called to Rebecca. 'Right – *now*!'

Rebecca let go. The kite jittered in the air, and dived straight down onto the sand.

'Try again!' said Jack.

They tried again. This time a gust must have caught the kite for it rose and Jack ran, mouth open wide with delight.

'See that!' he cried.

'Don't let go of the string, will you,' called Caroline, as the kite soared.

Rebecca walked beside Caroline, watching the kite dreamily. 'I had an idea,' she began. She could feel her hands twitching anxiously.

'What's that then?' Caroline asked.

'I thought . . . maybe . . . if you sort things out with Mum – if you make up, then perhaps . . . perhaps we could all live here with you. Your house is big enough and it's so beautiful here . . . ' Rebecca's words petered out.

Caroline's face contorted. 'No, no – that would never work, I'm afraid.'

'But why?' Rebecca asked, instantly overwhelmed with disappointment. 'Why not? There's no drugs here – it will help Mum to be in a place like this.'

'First of all,' said Caroline, 'what's happened between me and your mum isn't going to be sorted out overnight. It's going to take time to rebuild a relationship that broke down so long ago and so painfully. You'll have to be patient with us.'

'But when you do,' said Rebecca, 'what about then?'

Caroline shook her head. 'There's another reason too. Your mother hates it here.'

'Hates it?' Rebecca repeated in surprise. 'But how can she? I love it – nobody could hate a place like this.'

Caroline smiled. 'You're more like me, Rebecca. Your mother's different. Life here is too sedate and gentle for her – that's why she went to London as soon as she was old enough. She started a course and dropped out after a term – but she didn't come back here. She said no way was she ever coming back to live here.

'And even if she did, she'd have a job to find work. The summer's okay but it's ever so quiet in winter. And although there's no drug-taking to speak of, there's also no professional support. Your mum's going to need a whole lot of support to stay off the drugs. It's only the start of the road for her – you'll have to be patient there too.'

Jack's kite swooped down. It came too low and floated onto the pebbles near the water's edge. Jack ran to fetch it before a wave caught it.

Caroline put a hand on Rebecca's shoulder. 'I should think you might need some support too. If you're worried about anything and you want to phone me, I'll be here for you – don't forget that. And I hope you and Jack will come and stay in the school holidays.'

'Really?' Rebecca's mood lifted instantly. At least that would be something to look forward to.

'Of course,' said Caroline. 'And Denise, your social worker, phoned me yesterday… '

Rebecca looked at Caroline in surprise.

'She said there's a group starting up for children whose parents have got drug problems. She said you might need somewhere – someone outside the family to talk to about things.'

Rebecca thought about this – a group for children whose parents have drug problems. That meant there were others – others like them. This had never occurred to her before. She'd thought they were the only ones. She wasn't sure if she wanted to meet them – go to this group. But it was comforting to know they existed. She had another listener of course, Charlie. She felt warm at the thought of him and how kind he had been.

They walked on. The wind behind them seemed to urge them forward.

'I'm thinking about moving house,' Caroline said suddenly.

'Moving?' Rebecca exclaimed. 'But I thought you said we could come and stay?'

Caroline laughed. 'If I do move, I won't go far – I'll

still be in Southwold, and I'll make sure there's plenty of room for you and Jack. It's just that I've spent the last fourteen years burying myself in my work, and pining for Neil. I think now it's time to move on.'

She looked down at her watch. 'And talking of time . . . you'd better wind up that kite string, Jack,' she called. 'It's time we went back and finished off your packing.'

Rebecca said a reluctant goodbye to the beach, taking a last, deep breath of sea air. Back at the house she finished packing and was on her way downstairs with her bag when the doorbell rang.

She opened it to find Charlie standing on the doorstep. 'I've come to say goodbye,' he said.

'I wish we weren't going,' said Rebecca, suddenly full of emotion.

'I know what it's like,' said Charlie. 'Every time I come to stay with Dad, I get attached to this place all over again. It's always hard to leave – but if you don't go, you can't come back. That's what Dad says to me. And you will come back, won't you?'

'Yes,' said Rebecca. 'Caroline might move house but she says there'll always be room for me and Jack to stay – and we can come in the school holidays.'

Charlie couldn't hide his relief. He grinned. 'Dad and Caroline are getting on well, aren't they? It'd be great if they make a go of it.'

Rebecca nodded. 'Caroline's been looking so happy.'

'Dad's pretty chirpy too,' said Charlie. 'How's your mum?'

'I think she's okay – it's hard to tell on the phone,'

said Rebecca. 'She'll be here soon. I hope she and Caroline can sort things out between them.'

'I'm going to miss you,' Charlie said unexpectedly. 'This has been the best summer – having you here.'

'I'll miss you too,' said Rebecca. 'Will you give me your address at your mum's?'

Charlie handed her a piece of paper with the address and phone number clearly written out. 'You can write yours on here,' he said, pulling a further piece of paper and a pen from his pocket.

Rebecca wrote it and handed it to him. Then Charlie pulled something else from his pocket. It was a tiny box.

'This is for you,' he said.

Rebecca opened it carefully. Inside was a silver chain with a tiny orange gemstone hanging from it.

'It's amber,' said Charlie. 'I found it on the beach and I got it polished up for you. What do you think?'

'It's beautiful,' Rebecca said, meeting his eyes. 'Thank you, Charlie.'

Then Charlie leant forward, and Rebecca suddenly realised he was going to kiss her.

Just at that moment, Jack appeared on the stairs. 'Was that the door? Is it Mum?'

'Not yet,' said Rebecca.

Jack saw Charlie and leapt down the last five stairs, pushing himself between them. 'Charlie!'

Rebecca stood back to let Jack says his goodbyes.

'Have you seen the book on castles that Caroline gave me?' Jack asked Rebecca. 'I can't find it anywhere.'

'Try the lounge,' she suggested.

Jack went, and Rebecca was left standing with

Charlie once more. She looked into his eyes – was he going to try kissing her again – or had the moment passed? Charlie leant forward, and his mouth met hers. They held each other tight and didn't let go for a long time.

Finally, Charlie stood back, grinning as he gazed into her eyes.

Rebecca smiled. 'We will stay in touch, won't we?'

'Yes,' said Charlie, 'I promise.'

When Charlie had left, Jack appeared in the hall with his book and rushed back upstairs to finish packing. Rebecca was still buzzing from the thrill of Charlie's kiss. She went to find Caroline, and was surprised to see that the door to the room of china figures was open. She peered round.

'Come in,' said Caroline. 'Doesn't she look beautiful?'

She was pointing to the new figurine, which had pride of place at the front of one table.

'They're all lovely,' said Rebecca, 'especially that one.'

'When I move, I'm going to buy glass cabinets to put them in,' said Caroline. 'Bill was right – they'll be safer that way and easier for dusting. It's much more practical. I've decided to stop collecting now, as well. This one will be my last.'

'Why?' asked Rebecca.

'I think I have enough, don't you?'

'Maybe,' said Rebecca.

'They've been the centre of my life, all these years, you know,' Caroline explained. 'I enjoyed collecting them right from the start – when my mother bought me my first one.' Caroline pointed to a small figurine.

'Neil bought me Arabella after we were engaged. I loved her – she was my favourite, just as he was. Then when he and your mother ran off . . . I was so humiliated. I hid myself away.'

Caroline eyes were glazed. She looked dreamy. 'There was no one I could talk to,' she continued. 'So I talked to her – Arabella. I told her everything – poured out all my fury with your mother. There was something so life-like about Arabella – she seemed to take it all in – as if she was really listening. I even thought her expression changed sometimes.'

Caroline's face suddenly reddened. 'I don't know why I've told you all that,' she said with embarrassment. 'It must sound crazy to you.'

Rebecca felt a peculiar tingle go through her body. She thought about the china head – the strange things that had happened, the dreams. She looked up from the china figures and met Caroline's eyes.

'No,' she said finally. 'It doesn't sound crazy at all.'